CW00435111

Six Stories of

Love, Hate,

&

Other Weirdness

Micheal James Bradley

ISBN- 9798398551853

Publisher: Blue Glass Books
Cover design by: M.J.Bradley/AI
Printed in the United Kingdom and United States of
America

The ramblings and rants disguised as literature in the following pages are dedicated equally and variously to:

My family on Earth and elsewhere, the cool wise woman (with the tiny plastic hand, water for the table and all the best music), and anyone who gets something good, however small, from the following pages.

"This is where we are at right now, as a whole. No one is left out of the loop. We are experiencing a reality based on a thin veneer of lies and illusions. A world where greed is our God and wisdom is sin, where division is key and unity is fantasy, where the ego-driven cleverness of the mind is praised, rather than the intelligence of the heart."

BILL HICKS

For those who don't have the time or inclination to read this collection of stories in its entirety, the point or message of this book, if there *is* one (and only if you're the kind of reader who absolutely insists, for whatever reason, that there really *must* be a point to it) is: be honest. As little as the world encourages it these days, for better or worse – be yourself. Always. Life is too short, or too long, for anything else.

Except for when people are chasing you for something, obviously. Then it's better to pretend to be anyone else. Or hide, maybe. But in general: be yourself. And that, pretty much, is that.

Contents:

Truth Time

"Still got six minutes," Adam muttered, glancing at the antique-styled, neon-blue clock face glowing on his otherwise black phone screen. He blew out a slow lungful of air as a wave of nervous adrenaline tossed through his stomach and pulsed in his throat.

"Shouldn't be a problem if I'm careful," he thought aloud, calming slightly and staring at the untouched plate of cold toast in front of him on the kitchen table.

'Truth Time'.

The words churned his stomach every time they entered his head, and he pushed the plate out of reach.

The only reason he didn't take part in the trials with Abigail last August, he claimed at the time, was that it just seemed...well; scary. He recalled arguing with her that the technology was still "too new" back then; how sticking a gadget in your ear and having your private, inner thoughts automatically spoken, unfiltered, felt less like a social media trend and more like his worst nightmare.

He swiped his phone open. A concerned look fell on his face as he flicked through three apps of social media and inboxes full of excited messages. The words: 'Truth Time' leapt out at him in every post, hashtag, message and meme that he saw. Grotesque cartoons of the 'mind-reading' device that Adam would soon be reluctantly wearing portrayed it coming to life and wrapping around the user's throat. He saw images of politicians and television celebrities flashing smiles and peace signs as they clamoured to join and promote the event.

Each image he saw was bolstered by dozens of likes, hearts and thumb emojis of agreement. Adam exhaled hard again. What the hell was he letting himself in for?

"The big day!" sang Abigail as she entered the kitchen, almost dancing as she walked, and breaking Adam's thought with her voice. Standing still with her face suddenly solemn, she held her hand high as if swearing a courtroom oath: "I promise to tell the truth, the whole truth,

and...something, something, erm, so help me God, ha-ha! Oh, I'm so excited!" She beamed. "How do I look?" she asked Adam, without giving him time to answer, "I wanted to wear something...nice for 'Truth Time'. I mean, I know it's only the girls at work, and we all get on fine, but..." her eyes darted to her watch, which lit up to display '08.54' with a sudden flick of her right wrist, while her left hand gave another check of her left ear to ensure the gadget was fitted securely.

"You look beautiful," interrupted Adam, with a smile and tone he knew she adored, "As beaut...no, actually...more beautiful than the day I met you, in fact," he added, raising the camera on his phone to face her as if following a silent instruction.

It wasn't always those specific words he used to

respond to that routine morning question, but it was always worded along that line. Sometimes, he would say: "....It's like I'm falling in love for the first time again," or the equally routine: "You look what you are: the most beautiful woman I ever saw". He would then hold his fixed but natural-looking smile and wait for her automatic "Aww, baaaabe," response each time.

"Aww," Abigail answered, screwing up her nose in a way that Adam always insisted made his stomach flip, "Baaaabe, you're perfect, you are. But no cameras darlin'; I've not done my nails yet."

She turned sideways and bent her knees slightly, inviting Adam to look at the gadget in her left ear. "Look at my green light, babe," she asked, "am I 'Solid Green Line' or 'Rhythmic Pulse'? The instructions on the app said I should be on 'Rhythmic Pulse' by now, but upstairs I was on 'Flashing Orange', oh, I don't want it to mess up now. It worked perfectly when I tested it."

Adam nodded and put his phone back in his pocket. "You're 'Rhythmic Pulse'," he confirmed after leaning forward and squinting at her left ear, "All good to go."

Abigail smiled. "Ah, good," she said, reaching a bottle of nail varnish from the drawer beneath the sink, "That means I'm in 'Receive-slash-Transmit Mode'. You are too," she said, nodding at Adam's earpiece as it lay on the kitchen table, pulsing a smooth, green light, in a rhythm that looked like a heartbeat.

Adam quickly slid the phone from his pocket to check the time again. Three minutes to go.

"I was just reading about it," Adam revealed, with a

3

smile instead of a more honest frown, "Everybody's having a go at this, aren't they?" he said. "Shops, offices, schools, celebrities, politicians, even world leaders, Ab, it's huge!". His more honest frown duly swept away the smile as Adam reflected on his own words. "It's…. scary," he muttered.

"Hmm, yeah," confirmed Abigail, as she hastily but precisely painted her nails over the kitchen sink, "Everybody is getting involved. It's since the developers of the technology said they'd donate the money to charity, or something. Or some money, anyway. Someone's donating something, somewhere. Or something. I don't know. But the world's been through a lot, Adam, lockdowns and isolation; the last few years have been crazy. Maybe everyone's just looking for something real! Or a bit of togetherness! Or...feeling united by something fun for once instead of fear or worry. Everybody just letting everything out with this, instead of bottling it all up. Removing the social masks we wear, everybody just being genuine. A bit of honesty in the world, for once."

Adam laughed, scooping his cold toast into the bin while Abigail frantically flapped her drying nails over the sink. "Idiot," he thought. His stomach flipped again as his focus was distracted by the pulsing green light above her ear. He breathed heavily and wondered if this was exactly the kind of thought that would fall from his mouth uncontrollably when 'Truth Time' began. He swallowed hard, and briefly questioned again what the hell he was letting himself in for.

"Well I don't know if honesty is the best way to have fun!" he said, distracting from the thought,

4

grabbing his phone again and tapping the screen until it shone into action. "It says here that the divorce rate increased by 20 per cent and redundancies by 30 per cent during the trial run. Too much honesty seems a bit...well...scary, don't you think?"

Abigail turned, screwing up her mouth in a disappointed curve, "What do you mean, 'honesty is scary'?" she said, extending a freshly-painted fingernail towards him in a joking threat. "Ohhh, I get it," she said in a sarcastic tone, "My sweet, poor little idiot, you still think 'Truth Time' is going to fry your brain, hmm? Is that it? Or, a shadowy elite alien government is going to farm your silly thoughts and stick them on a computer, and steal your boring identity or whatever your conspiracy sites say, is that it?"

"Alright, alright," replied Adam, sitting back at the kitchen table, "And no, actually, I don't think anyone is going to steal my boring thoughts or whatever you said. I'm just...it seems a bit...scary. Like, aren't we honest enough? Do we really need a gadget to force us into being honest? I've got nothing to hide in my life...it just feels like...like you don't trust me or something, making us play this."

Abigail rolled her eyes and sighed, "Babe, nobody is calling anybody a liar, ok? We've been through this. We went through this last year, for God's sake. 'Truth Time' isn't about exposing people. It's about tapping into your subconscious, connecting with that instead of...instead of all this surface stuff we all pretend is real."

"Oh, so I'm not a liar, I'm superficial, am I? That's great, that's fine then I suppose." Adam interrupted, half-joking.

"Oh, come on, Adam, stop it," corrected Abigail, "I didn't say 'you', I said 'we', as in, 'us', as in; people. Society. Humans, y'know? Our plastic little fake world…it's about bringing us all together, as individuals, by encouraging us to be our inner selves."

Adam stared back at Abigail blankly. "And which part," he said with a raised eyebrow, "of every word that you just said, does not sound like the most terrifying thing anyone has ever said?"

"Babe," pleaded Abigail, nodding at the kitchen table with arched eyebrows, indicating that Adam should pocket his phone again, "For me. Play along for me. Is your device in?"

"Yes," Adam smiled, tapping the small, white device he had placed in his ear while he toyed with his phone, "Left ear, charged up, I've read my leaflet," he added with a sarcastic smile.

"Aw good," smiled Abigail, "And don't worry! Just go about your day. Act normal. Don't try and control what you are going to say; you won't be able to. The device will tap into your subconscious and those words or images will come right from your mouth the moment they appear in your head. Just try and go about your day at work as normal, and don't worry about it too much. It'll all be back to normal by five o'clock. Or maybe six."

Adam laughed, "Sorry, what? Ab, I think about some very weird stuff, sometimes…like…weird little rhymes I make up or… or maybe I'll get to work and instantly start giving detailed, individual descriptions to everyone at work about how much they secretly bore or irritate me. I bottle those thoughts for a

6

reason, Ab! What if I start saying them aloud in a meeting or something? I'll lose my job! What if people do that to me?"

Abigail giggled. "Relax, idiot," she said. "It will be fine. You'll see. Last year was a laugh, all the girls at work, gossiping and acting like children. It was fun! And the research behind it is....ohmyGODtensecondstogo!" she suddenly screamed, interrupting herself.

"What?!!" Adam yelled back, eyes wide with panic, "Ten seconds? Oh God, Ab, I don't feel ready..."

"Four...three..." beamed Abigail, eyes fixed on her tiny gold watch. The final passing seconds seemed to each last for a full minute to Adam. He screwed his eyes tightly shut as soon as he heard Abigail's excited voice shriek the word: "One...", in anticipation of the unknown.

Adam waited a moment, then slowly opened his eyes to see Abigail, grinning with delight.

"Welcome to 'Truth Time' babe! Yaaay!" she cheered, punching a fist in the air. "Adam Jones I love you!" she squealed excitedly. The device behind her ear gave a slight, warm beep and a green pulse of confirmation met her words.

"Woohoo," stated Adam, flatly.

Abigail scooped paperwork from the table into her briefcase and headed to the door. "Right, I'm late for work. And, thank you, babe. This means a lot to me." she said, still smiling as the device behind her ear let out its second affirmative beep. Her eyes lit up with delight at the sound; at the scientific confirmation of her love for Adam, at the fact that 'Truth Time' had begun. Turning excitedly, she headed out of the door, and off to work.

Adam lifted his hand to his left ear with the delicacy of a bomb disposal expert going for the final wire cut. He lightly touched the device. It let out a double beep at the contact from his fingertip, and Adam shot his hand back down to his side. "Woah," he whispered to himself, "It's started."

Walking to the living room, Adam reached for his phone again. This time, along with the hashtags and cartoons, his timeline was filled with eager, initial updates from other participants around the globe.

Sarcastic memes had largely been replaced by images of smiling crowds, standing in the shape of a globe or a heart, all holding hands and proudly displaying their beeping, flashing left ears. Positive messages: quotes about the importance of honesty and trust and being yourself, now outnumbered the worried jokes.

He opened a new message with the 'Sender' name of 'Satan'. It was Adam's boss. The message was a response to an earlier message Adam had sent as soon as he woke at 6.30 am, complaining and apologising in dramatic tones about a mysterious cough he had suddenly developed and that while it didn't require medical attention, he regrettably felt that he needed the day away from work. It ended with another apology and a flourish of emojis depicting various states of ill health.

"No problem fella," read the predicted reply: "Come in later if you feel well, hope you feel better tomorrow," accompanied by a flourish of thumbs-up emojis.

"Gullible tit," said Adam aloud to himself, "No wonder your wife's sleeping with your business partner." In his momentary bubble of elation at avoiding work for the day, Adam didn't notice those words fall out automatically and without intention from his lips, aloud. He didn't notice the device around his ear beeping its first satisfied tone at completing its duty and revealing his inner thought.

Sinking into the sofa and switching on the tv, Adam smiled as he realised how easy 'Truth Time' would be after all. The whole day at home. Abigail busy at work. His eyes lit up. "Nobody will hear anything!", he laughed aloud, "Oh my God, this will be easy! Ha! Ab will be back tonight when it's over, and everybody at work thinks I'm on my deathbed. Perfect!"

The clock on the tv screen said: 9:10 am, and Adam grinned. Glancing around the room, his eyes found the photograph that hung above the television, showing Abigail and Adam on their wedding day, surrounded by Abigail's family. Adam felt his face fall into the routine fake smile he made whenever Abigail drew his attention to the image during quiet moments in their evenings, such as tv show commercial breaks, or at the end of arguments. "Ahh, Ab," Adam sighed while still smiling, before casually but very unexpectedly continuing with the words: "Your mother is such an interfering bitch."

His eyes widened as the secret opinion left his lips. His hand instinctively shot across his mouth in shock. "What the..." Adam gasped, as his eyes fell from the photograph and the device in his left ear let out a brief, affirmative beep.

He let his hand fall slowly from his mouth and stood up quickly. "Ok, Adam exactly what the hell did you just say?" he asked himself in a cautious

9

tone as his eyes fell back to the television.

The scenes his eyes were met with were drastically different to those of a few moments ago. The sound was low, Adam couldn't hear, and in his bewildered state, he didn't think of increasing the volume. The pictures spoke for themselves, though. First, he saw a minor politician, mostly known for his appearances on celebrity shows, looking guilty and defensive in an interview. But that didn't look like anything new or strange.

Next came a clip of a fight. Adam's eyes widened in shock as the politician's interview was replaced by a video of him being punched as he opened his front door five minutes ago. A small crowd of people stood around him with mobile phones pointed at the fight, holding placards of protest that Adam couldn't quite decipher. Behind all of their ears, the small device that Adam wore was calmly flashing its now-familiar, bright green pulse as the tv gang's plans for peaceful chants of protest were instantly replaced by a rapid wave of true thoughts, swelling to slurs and verbal abuse, and then violence in the moment that Truth Time began.

The politician lay bleeding and the crowd's cheers and chants could be heard even at low volume. As quickly as it came, the scene cut to a flurry of men and women variously on bended knee, proposing to partners who were responding by either breaking down in tears of surprised joy or running away. Just as quickly, the footage cut back to the earlier image of children standing in the shape of a heart, smiling.

"What the hell is happening? The world is going crazy," Adam gasped as his hand delicately touched the device in his ear and his eyes fell back to the photograph above the television, "And Abigail's dad is a pretentious snob with a bad haircut and bad cholesterol and I wish he'd die... oh my God!" he exclaimed again, as his wave of fear intensified.

Adam fell back into the sofa. "Christ, it's only been ten minutes, how big is this thing going to get?" he thought, as his mind quickly filled with visions of political arguments and nuclear war.

"Get a grip, Adam," he ordered himself, folding his arms as he began trying to evaluate his situation. "I'm home alone," he re-confirmed, his eyes scanning the room as he spoke, "I'm home alone all day...I'll speak to nobody...just...don't answer the phone! That's it! Just don't answer the phone and I'll be ok! It'll all be over by five. All back to normal."

His face broke into a relieved smile and he lay back on the sofa to digest his masterplan. "Ah, I'm gonna be fine," he laughed, "Just don't move, just watch tv and then tonight I can tell Abi and everyone that I've had a day of awakening, or something. A 'new me', or whatever. Ah, this is actually going to be brilliant," he laughed again, spreading out further on the sofa, "Nobody's going to know a..."

In what seemed like a millisecond, a key prodded at the front door lock. It swung open and Abi stood there, furious, dishevelled, and frowning.

"Aaaaargh!" she screamed before the door slammed closed with a bang that rattled the windows. "Screw people and screw work and screw everything!" she added as if clarifying her roar.

"Oh God no! You're home!" Adam said as the earpiece let out another beep at successfully intercepting a thought. The words were spoken in complete disappointment and dread at seeing her

11

return but were interpreted as love and empathy by Abigail; of recognising her distress.

"What are you doing here? Don't you feel well? Ugh, that woman!" said Abigail, marching across the apartment to the kitchen and pouring a coffee from the still-warm pot. She continued her subconscious but audible rant, "Same bitch every day! Pushes in the queue at the bus stop! Thinks she looks great and can do what she wants! Well I told her babe, I told her that I wasn't going to stand for it, and she said something back and I just screamed in her face! Oh my God, I'm shaking! This crazy gadget, oh my God!" Her wide-eyed expression fell into a frown as it settled back to Adam, "Why are you home babe?" she repeated.

"Why don't you go back to work?" said Adam in a shocked and desperate response. Again, it was a plea that was interpreted by Abigail as a concern.

"Aww, babe, I think you're so sweet," she gushed, as the device in her ear beeped a confirmation, "No, they're ok with me staying home. I called them and explained what happened and I got through to the nice receptionist instead of that little bitch who thinks she owns the place… you know, the one I was a bridesmaid for." Abigail's hand shot across her mouth in a gesture that Adam himself was already familiar with performing, "Oops," she giggled, "Listen to me, I'm the bitch!"

"I messaged my boss and told him that I felt really ill, but I'm fine," said Adam, answering Abigail's earlier question automatically without a filter. His face froze at the confession, and it suddenly reminded Abigail of a guilty schoolboy. "Babe! Abigail gasped in horror, "What did he say?" Oh,

12

Adam! That's not like you! Lying to your boss!"

"It is," admitted Adam without wanting to, "It's exactly like me. I do it all the time…anyway he just replied with: "ok" and some thumb emojis. He doesn't care; too busy following his wife when she sneaks off with every guy she meets. She's secretly with his business partner today. I got roped in to send her a message to meet him at a hotel. He knows she's up to something. Says he'll shoot them both when he catches them. They're pathetic."

"Babe!" exclaimed Abigail again, surprised, "What are you talking about? I thought we got on with Christopher and his wife? And you're lying? You're lying to your boss about his wife's affair? What?"

"Nope, you get on with them, because you just smile at everyone you meet until they like you. I can't stand the bloke, personally." said Adam, now visibly embarrassed by his own revelations, with the truth cascading from his mouth as soon as it formed in his mind. "I hate everybody there, Ab," he continued rapidly and without emotion, "I just pretend I like it so you don't ask me about work, because then I have to ask you about your dull job, and I couldn't care less. But I've never told you that because you'd moan,

and your voice irritates me when you moan. And you moan every day."

They stared at each other, numb in the sudden silence.

"What…did…you…just…say?" Abigail tearfully asked, with Adam's words ringing around their heads like an unexpected fire alarm.

Adam continued uncontrollably, "I said I hate talking about work because I hate work. And talking to you is boring." They both gasped as the truth fell from his lips. Abi sobbed suddenly. "I knew this would happen!" shrieked Adam, before running into the bathroom opposite, slamming the door behind him.

Abigail was motionless, staring at the bathroom door. Adam's back was pressed firmly against the other side, and he felt a wave of sweat consume him. The mirrored wall to his left reflected his panic, causing him to breathe heavily. He reached for his ear, and the device let out its already-familiar 'do-not-touch' tone on contact. "What...just...happened?" he said aloud, as soon as the thought entered his head.

On the other side of the door, Abigail was striding towards his hiding spot. She approached with the usual natural tenderness she gave these situations; times when Adam had said something to offend her and walked away, leaving her feeling inexplicably guilty until she made up with him.

She gently slid her hand towards the door handle as usual and opened her mouth to begin her routine, soft-voiced attempt at making up. Instead, the device in her left ear beeped as it detected a true thought and the words: "Boring? Smile at people until they like me? You liar! Open this door right now!" roared from her lips, surprising them both.

Adam lunged forward and began to pace the bathroom. He heard Abigail's stilettoed stomp fade slightly until it reached the living room carpet and turned to a dull thud. A few moments of silence followed. And then, in a scream that genuinely shook Adam, he heard: "And why the hell is our wedding picture turned to face the wall? Adam?

14

Adaaaam? You answer me right now!!"

Adam fell back against the bathroom door again and slid to the floor. "Because I hate your parents and they've ruined my life and I never wanted to marry you," he screamed unpreventably, his hand gripping his mouth as tightly as the device gripped his ear, but still the words echoed around Abigail.

He glanced at his phone. 9.29 am. Less than thirty minutes. Less than half an hour since 'Truth Time' began; his life was over. His marriage was over. His whole world was over. On his phone, the image of the heart-shaped children filled his screen again, and he let out another scream as he slammed it back in his pocket.

Silently standing, careful not to squeak or creak or make a sound, he walked to the waist-height window directly opposite him. Sweating heavily, trapped in the bathroom with Abigail's angry gaze still burning through the door and directly into the back of his head, he glanced through the window. "I'm getting the hell out of here," he said aloud, unwillingly. The device let out a calm beep, instantly followed by Adam's spoken thought: "Oh Christ she can hear everything! Oh God just shut up, Adam!"

"I can hear you, you stupid bastard," confirmed Abigail with another scream through the door, "Who the hell are you Adam? Who the hell are you?"

"I'm escaping out of the window," Adam shouted back automatically, "I don't want to face you and I'm running away out of the bathroom window oh for the love of God how do I turn this thing off?"

"Adam!" Abi screamed again.

"What?" shouted Adam, as he guided his leg through the window.

"Come back! Stop it!" she shrieked.

"No!" he repeated, as his second leg raised through the window frame, "I'm not even sorry, oh shut up Adam, I don't love you Abi! Argh I hate this!"

"Adam if you don't stop it, we're over! You can pack your bags and go!"

Abigail screamed his name several times again, but all she could hear was the loose latch on the open bathroom window frame as it swung in the breeze.

On the outside of the bathroom wall, Adam gasped for breath as his heart raced and his eyes darted in all directions. He had no idea what was happening, absolutely no idea where he was going, and, somewhat more importantly; no way to even begin processing what the hell just happened with Abi. He briefly placed his hands on his knees, still gasping, with Abi's screams and bangs on the bathroom door still raging behind him.

His mind flashed back to kissing Abi 'goodbye' only thirty minutes ago. The hidden truths that had unwillingly poured out in that short time since 'Truth Time' began made that kiss feel like a lifetime ago. Now here he was - standing in his garden, probably homeless, definitely loveless, and if everybody who'd gone to work was going through the same thing, probably jobless any moment now, too. "All because of the truth," he stammered, in disbelief.

He darted to the garden gate and began walking sharply away from the house. "I need to think," he said aloud as he gazed at the pavement, "I just need to..." his thoughts were broken by a new scream.

"I don't care!" a woman's voice screeched, "I am sick to death of sneezing every morning!" Adam's

16

eyes followed the sound. On the opposite pavement, at the end of the garden of some wealthy, long-married neighbours whom Adam had never spoken to, there stood a slim, tall woman, the homeowner, next to an open bin. In her outstretched hands, she held an obese, wailing, ginger cat. Behind her ear, Adam could make out the already-familiar green pulse of the 'Truth Time' device.

"Stop it you lunatic!" bellowed a wheezing male voice. It was followed by the figure of an equally obese, older man in an expensive-looking bathrobe, trotting down the long gravel driveway towards the bin. "Don't...don't you dare," he puffed, purple-faced and barely running.

"Shut up, Jeremy," the tall woman drawled matter-of-factly, "I'm not taking allergy tablets anymore just so that this little fat demon can scratch my face and shit in my shoes every morning. I've always hated it, and now it's going." With those words, she promptly dropped the screaming cat into the bin and slammed the lid closed, before folding her arms and staring at her husband. "And don't run, you fat old fool," she added in a disgusted tone, as the poor bewildered man drew to a heaving halt, "God, look at you, you can barely breathe."

The man, whose ears were the first Adam had seen that morning not being gripped by the device, fell to his knees and began to weep, staring at the woman in genuine shock. Adam stared too and they briefly made eye contact as the woman continued to casually detail her own extramarital affairs and one-night-stands to the man on the floor, while the device throbbed calm confirmations behind her ear. Genuine tears rolled down her face and her head

17

shook in helpless horror while her own true feelings and secrets, buried so deep and hidden so well for so many years, rolled from her lips, without force but against her will.

Other loud voices filled the air now, both near and distant: arguments, breakups, disputes, unwanted surprises, unsuppressed honesty. Adam began to run, then sprint; further down the street and towards the town, trying to escape the sounds.

The first few streets were strangely quiet for the time of morning. No school-run traffic, no late commutes, and no early shoppers. Adam suspected that the scene he was fleeing was being played out in every other home, too.

The few people he passed were all wearing the device, and all muttering thoughts and truths as they made their way to wherever. A woman wearing earphones with music blasting into them muttered: "I hate my face, I hate my life, I hate my hair," like a mantra as she gave Adam a smiling, convincing, stranger's nod to indicate 'good morning', oblivious to her own words.

"Nobody's ever going to find out where they are," said a sweetly-smiling old man aloud to nobody as Adam raced by, "Nobody's ever going to suspect a thing." The tone of the words sounded sinister, menacing almost, in a way that completely betrayed his friendly face and smart clothes. Adam ran faster. The closer he got to the town centre, the more voices he heard in every direction. A slow-building tsunami of honesty was now flooding through every street at full, unstoppable force.

The unexpected nightmare that complete honesty brought with it spouted from the mouths of everyone

18

he saw, everyone he heard. He was already becoming familiar with the sight of women and men standing on their doorsteps or gardens, with a partner leaning from a window and throwing down clothes and suitcases while they shouted at each other. He was getting strangely used to the sight of perfectly average-looking people ranting or wailing as they walked dogs or pushed prams. Others, in fact, most, he noticed, were making strange noises as they walked… childlike noises or grunts or ticks as their subconscious thoughts gushed out. A stern-faced businessman, striding with a briefcase, made strange baby sounds and gurgling noises as he stepped inside a high-bricked office. Amused onlookers laughed at the sight, while they themselves helplessly spilled out their own strange

sounds and inner diatribes. A younger man in a suit pushed swiftly past the crowd. His hand cradled his head in shock and self-surprise as he calmly spoke

into his phone to inform the caller that he was stealing from the charity he worked for, altering accounts and siphoning donations into his own bank.

Adam's hand raised to his ear as the madness overwhelmed him. He gripped the device quickly to try and tear it from his head. The moment the gadget sensed the additional pressure in his fingertips, a searing pain shot through Adam's skull; a sudden electric-like burning so intense that he instinctively removed his touch with a loud yell of agony, and the pain instantly subsided.

"Christ," he panted, lightly touching his head again to make sure the pain didn't return. Adam glanced at the time. Still, around eight hours to go. Maybe nine.

But then what? What was life going to be like when 'Truth Time' was switched back this evening? The sudden thought snowballed in his mind. He wondered how many more couples, families and friendships around the town...the country...the whole world, for God's sake, were, right now, ending because everyone was finally being completely honest with each other?

His head filled with visions of chaos around the globe; people's entire lives crumbling because of the automatic thoughts falling from their mouths. The insults and "screw you" rants that would, right now, be playing out instead of fake smiles and "good mornings" in the workplace of every despised job and home and two-faced social interaction.

"The world's ending," he said with an uncontrollable cry, as birds calmly sang their songs in the trees and the sun shone through a blue, unbothered sky. No bombs, no death, but the world felt like it was ending. He suddenly thought of Abi crying.

Maybe...maybe this was all for the best?" he heard his voice say aloud, "In the long run, I mean. Yes, life with Abi is safe. Future-proof. But I'm never going to be happy. I already know that. I never wanted that life," his audible thoughts continued, adding a new voice to the mad crowd, "I don't want to live from holiday to holiday, from Facebook 'Like' to Facebook 'Like'. And I really don't want her vile parents every Sunday, or Abigail slowly turning us into a clone of her parents."

He didn't want that life. He knew it long before 'Truth Time'. He didn't love Abi. He'd known that for a long time.

He thought of the politician on tv, of all of the politicians; every one of them across the world. Maybe it was time for them to let out all of their lies. Maybe all the secretly violent people attacking them needed exposing. Maybe it was all for the best so that tomorrow the world can be a more honest place?

He thought of every fake friendship or dead relationship ending and every real one starting. All at once, all over the world; one unprecedented outburst of genuine conversation and honesty.

The rosy images forming in his mind were shattered by the screech of a car grinding to a halt. The car door slammed and by the time Adam's already-bewildered brain could comprehend the scene, the driver was running into the road towards the now-busy, mid-morning traffic. Vehicles zigzagged to avoid him, but rather than dodge their moves, it appeared that the man was trying to intercept their high-speed swerves.

"Hit me, hit me!" The man wailed to speeding motorists as he frantically lunged at their vehicles, "I can't stand this, I can't do this anymore!", he continued, as his left ear pulsed a steady green flash of agreement. Adam stared closely at the man's ear and saw blood and deep scratches, or knife cuts, from a failed attempt to remove the flashing gadget.

The man turned again, sprinting back across the road in Adam's direction, eyes closed, audibly praying for collision. Despite what looked like his best efforts to die, the man stumbled, weeping, onto the pavement a few feet from where Adam stood.

Adam froze. The man was ranting at high-speed. His words were hard to make out between sobs and cries, but Adam felt like he didn't need to hear them. He felt as though he was looking at himself. He felt as though he was looking at everyone, all over the world. 'Truth Time' wasn't going to unite the planet, he realised as the man continued to break down in front of him. The complete truth is the last thing everyone needs if their private worlds are going to keep spinning.

The chaotic high street was now filled with torn voices as every subconscious thought continued pouring out. Occasional cries of pain whenever people tried to remove the device. Their screams punctuated the audible inner monologues of everyone around Adam; rants of hate, roared-out declarations of existential dread, hidden guilts and strange noises. Cars whizzed by but the man on the floor was too exhausted to move now.

Another voice distracted Adam. Somewhere distant to his right. He turned to see a short, plain-looking woman, perhaps somewhere in her late fifties, running down the pavement towards them.

She was talking. Not shouting. The words weren't clear at first, but Adam could tell she was repeating something. As she grew closer, he noticed tears in her eyes. The device behind her ear was duly giving its calm, affirmative pulse.

"Truth Time, Truth Time, Truth Time," the mantra suddenly became clear above the roaring traffic as she ran faster towards where Adam stood. Her eyes, now clearly visible, were fixed on the broken soul kneeling on the pavement. As Adam began to realise what was about to happen, the woman charged into the weeping man, using her full weight to shove him into the oncoming, endless traffic, her words repeating non-stop with her tears as she did so.

A car dragged to a halt as it rolled over his body, and people screamed as the woman continue her run down the street without pause, her constant words and flailing arms eventually lost to the noise and swell of the crowd.

Adam stumbled into the suddenly-still carnage. Cries filled the air more than words now, as more people frantically tried in vain to rip the devices from their ears. Running again, he made his way through the crowded street and instinctively to the only place he knew; back home.

Arriving, he saw the bathroom window was still open. Abigail hadn't been in there, he reasoned. Exhausted, he approached the front door, retrieved the spare key from beneath the doormat, and walked inside.

The house was silent. Instantly noticeable was the complete absence of any object, trinket or picture belonging to Abigail. She'd gone. He had expected as much. The television set was still playing the rolling news. Adam sank back into the sofa. He glanced at the time on the tv screen; five hours to go. Maybe six. Maybe forever.

The newsreader from earlier had gone. Presumably another victim to some insane or honest outburst. Adam questioned for a moment if there was really any difference between insanity and honesty. The thought was broken by a return to the image of the children, smiling in their heart shape, who had been so optimistic at 9 am at the prospect

23

of a new, honest world that was about to arrive.

He pictured what that photograph would look like if it were taken now. They'd all be crying for a start; they'll know by now that there's no Santa Claus. Some of them would know their parents didn't love or even like each other. Some more of them would have seen their mothers or fathers or both, rushing down the street, pushing each other under traffic or ranting about how much they secretly hate their lives.

Abigail wouldn't be back, Adam thought to himself, as his stare turned to a blurry haze. Again, he felt terrified and elated.

He muted the television and sighed harder than he had all morning. He blinked hard, several times, and laughed, but he didn't know why. He knew the full chaos of the day would register with him sometime soon, but it hadn't yet. He tried to think of the future, of 'Truth Time' ending in a few hours. But he didn't know what to imagine.

He couldn't imagine what was going to follow, he realised. He knew it would be hell, though; he knew that whatever happened next, for him and everyone, nothing would ever be the same again. "People need lies," he thought in a loud, clear voice. "People need their inner world kept private if they're not going to sound crazy, and people need lies.

"Not big lies," he clarified to himself, "Not deceitful ones about who you are and what people really do or don't mean to you. Not lies about feelings." He looked routinely for the wedding picture above the television. A perfect rectangle of dust and a picture hook was all that remained of it. He stared at the space where the photograph had been hanging. "I even hate their dust," he giggled to himself, as the device let out a small, calm, affirmative beep and Adam suddenly felt like crying.

"Honesty." he concluded, his voice quivering as tears formed, "We all just need honesty when things are good, and honesty when things are bad. It shouldn't send us crazy. We shouldn't bottle things up. That's what all of this is."

Adam sighed, exhausted. His wet eyes raised to the television again, already numb to whatever stark image might be there. The screen responded with the image of the children, standing in their heart shape, ears optimistically glowing green.

He didn't hear the unlocked door creak open. He heard it slam shut, however, and he turned his head to face Abi.

Except, he didn't see Abi. Instead, he saw his boss. Instantly Adam's thoughts flew to his early morning message, reluctantly reciting it as his mind scanned the memory for any insults or slurs. "You're called 'Satan' on my phone, Chris," said Adam, involuntarily revealing his inner thought while visibly cringing with genuine guilt at his own words.

The man before him looked too angry to care. He was crying too, but his swollen red eyes suggested he had been crying for some time. Adam's face looked genuinely apologetic as he continued to verbalise his awkward trail of thought, "But I do hate you and I hate my job and I didn't want to come to work. I never do," he said, as the gadget duly beeped.

The confession didn't even register with the intruder. Reaching for his pocket, he pulled out a small pistol, aiming it at Adam's head. "It's you, isn't it,", he stuttered between tears, "My w…wife… some... someone's sleeping with her, aren't they, I saw the message you sent…a hotel...it's...it's...you". The last word left his lips in a roar.

Adam had time to say, "Chris, it's your business part..." before a single bullet from the gun flew across the room, directly through the centre of Adam's forehead, and settled deep in the wall behind him, where Abigail's graduation photograph had been hanging a few hours earlier. "Liar," said the still-crying man, staring at the lifeless body before him. The device behind Adam's ear turned to a steady, unresponsive, orange glow, and a second gunshot echoed through the room, through the window, and out into the chaotic street, where it blended seamlessly with the sirens and the screams beneath an already exploding sky.

The Silent Ballad of
Zoe Malone

The day had sped by.

No sooner had offices closed and shops shut their doors than the people who had been frowning at screens and fake-smiling with customers all day had gone to bed, ready to do it all over again in the morning.

Along the empty streets created by this ritual, Zoe was making her way through the night and across the town. She was still wearing the "formal yet *in*formal" clothes that Department Head Jenny Reed insisted all staff must wear at the library. Zoe felt her retro blouses, clattering plastic bangles and gypsy skirts just about slotted into this holy regime, while allowing her a sense of individuality, a sense of rebellion.

The library had closed five hours ago at 7 pm, but Zoe had not been home yet.

Returning to her sparse little flat seemed to hold no real point. She found it impossible to switch off before the decent side of 2 am lately, and although

27

she prided herself on needing "remarkably little sleep, really", she knew full well that tomorrow morning she would *again* be sleepily sneaking in to work at around half-past nine, desperately hoping not to get caught.

Thoughts of her debatable choice of work clothes, images of Jenny Reed's turkey neck passionately wobbling as it croaked out orders, and the faint smell of those dreary, endless aisles of books were acting as a kind of pacemaker as Zoe steered herself through the inevitable imaginary stares and sense of being followed that accompany walking alone at night.

Within fifteen minutes or so of crossing near-empty roads and walking quickly past the few people she saw, Zoe turned down the now familiar side street. She smiled inwardly as she saw the all-night café shining its dismal light through the dirty window.

Zoe walked in through a door which she always expected to trigger off some kind of bell or chime, though it never did. So, looking at the floor, she gave her usual slight cough to compensate, always feeling inexplicably as if she had to announce her arrival.

Lightly pulling at the long leather strap on her shoulder bag, she walked to the booth at the far corner of the room and sat down. Zoe wanted this action to appear as cool as she saw it in her mind; assuming all eyes were on her, she placed her handbag onto the table and took out a silver-plated cigarette case and a scuffed silver lighter. She lit the cigarette and placed the handbag next to her thigh on the rounded, plastic bench before letting out two

28

slow, thin, perfect plumes of smoke from her nose, directly through the half-open window which acted as an outdoor smoking area.

But nobody saw. Nobody even glanced.

Zoe rested her elbows on the table and looked at the tin foil ashtray that sat slightly off-centre in front of her. It still contained the traces of black ash that she had seen here last night. The edges of the foil were still folded perfectly inwards where she had been playing with it a few nights ago. The almost recognisable letter 'Z' was still painted on the top-left corner of the table in dark-red pen. This was Zoe's table. Or so Zoe liked to tell herself.

She had been visiting the café almost nightly for seven weeks.

She'd arrive late, stay until around two-thirty, consider telephoning for a taxi, and then walk home.

Her latest fad.

The latest in a life-long line of fixations that appeared in Zoe's head in a heartbeat and, as soon as her mind had been fully consumed by them, left just as quickly.

Places, objects, and even *people* had all been subjected to the same fleeting, intense obsession in her mind, and all had been abandoned. And none of them, not even those long-forgotten people, had any real idea that Zoe even existed.

Her first visit to the café on an equally stormy night happened for no real reason other than Zoe's sudden compulsion to open the next door that she saw. A sudden feeling of being followed had overwhelmed her out of nowhere on that slow, reluctant walk home after work. By the time she first turned blindly down the now-familiar alley, her heart

29

pounded in her throat as she ran towards the dim orange light of the café. She gripped the copper door handle tightly and released it with a deep breath. Turning to look over her shoulder, she saw nobody lurking amongst the shadows and overflowing dustbins. Backing away slowly from the door, Zoe peered through the dirt-caked windows at the few blurred figures that sat inside and then continued her walk across the town.

When she returned the next evening, Zoe had waited outside in the alley for a good twenty minutes, debating whether to enter or not. Staring at the door, Zoe felt like a nervous new school pupil late for their first class, trying to summon the courage to turn the door handle and walk inside. Never once wondering why she felt the need to be there. Never once thinking about why she wanted to be anywhere but home, every moment of her life.

Finally entering, Zoe sat on one of the seats against the counter, ordered a single cup of black coffee and left after about an hour. Two nights later she returned, sat in the booth she was currently occupying, and stayed late.

Now, Zoe was desperate to consider herself a regular here.

She liked to think of the owner or his wife walking back into the kitchen and saying with a smile: "That lady's here again," before everyone in the kitchen joined them in a smile of contentment. Even at work, during the hated, mind-numbing duties of a job she had studied long and hard to get, her mind would flit more and more onto the café; how she would go there again that night after finishing work instead of taking her routine yet random ride across town on the first bus that she saw.

The image always appeared the same way in her mind.

She would walk into the café, sit at her regular seat, and light a cigarette. Other regulars would smile at her, but nervously since they were not here as often as she was. Later, maybe around 1 am, the owner, Ted, would walk over. Towel thrown over his shoulder, apron stained, and talk to Zoe about *everything*. They would exchange a few stories, laugh in the way that owners and regulars do, and then he would go back into the kitchen.

The problem was, none of this ever happened.

To the few customers who noticed her, Zoe appeared to be a self-conscious woman in her mid-thirties, nervous and shy. To the owners, she was just a customer who had started to come in for some odd reason; she certainly wasn't one of the truck drivers, off-duty nurses and other night shifters who usually occupied the booths. She was simply the plain-dressed lady, probably a secretary, who from her second visit had begun to get increasingly more over-familiar when ordering.

The café, if she'd have thought about it, was the last place on earth Zoe would be if she were ever able to think clearly. The one thing Zoe's mind had never been, though, was clear.

There was a constant cloud, as she would call it, a permanent analysis of every detail of every situation, past or present...

What *are* people thinking all the time?

All those times when she had made such a fool of herself by laughing too loudly, speaking without thinking or being called rude when she was *honestly* just answering their damn question...

What *are* people *thinking* about her?

And people can be so cruel…so…*cruel* that the very people she thought she could befriend would be the very people who were laughing about what an idiot she was right now, *right at this very*…

Zoe threw her head back sharply and inhaled loudly through her nose, as the sudden whirlwind of paranoia cleared.

She sat still for a few moments, then raised her eyes to see if her sudden jolt had caused concern – or amusement – among any of the other customers. It felt to her like a violent movement that could easily have startled someone.

But everyone was still checking their phones, still sitting alone reading, still leaving, still entering.

As usual, she had gone unnoticed.

Calmed, though only back down to her usual level of inner panic, she raised her hand to a passing waiter who stopped and took her order for a cup of sugarless black coffee.

In the time the waiter was gone, Zoe pulled the ashtray towards her. She was surprised that the foil rim was too secure in its new position to be bent back again. Next, she slid it along the width of the table until it covered the large letter 'Z'. To her eyes, the letter now looked almost *neon*...and so *hideously* obvious in fact that the waiter would instantly recognise her as the culprit. She'd told him her name enough times.

Quickly scanning the room for witnesses, Zoe 'casually' ensured that the offending letter could not possibly be viewed from any angle that the waiter was likely to return by. Calming herself slightly, she glanced at the kitchen door. Ted will be furious about this act of vandalism, she thought.

The thought caused her to frown. Maybe...just maybe...the only reason the letter had not been removed is because Ted and his wife are waiting for the criminal to return to the scene of the crime, and complete the name or offensive slogan, she thought, as her thoughts began to spiral. 'They' being the police, of course. They'll have to become involved at some stage. Ted will have to prosecute. He won't want to, but he'll have no choice. A crime is a crime. He would never have expected it of her – in fact, she's the last person he would have expected to have done such a mindless, terrible thing. And what if the police decide to throw the book at her? Make an example of her? Oh God, what if...

Zoe glanced around the room. No one had seen her move the ashtray. She was certain of it now. Just to be sure, though, she casually lowered her left arm and lay it across the table, completely obscuring any possible view of the ashtray from anyone else but herself.

Zoe glanced out of the nearest large window, situated awkwardly for her two booths down from where she was sitting. It had been raining, she was surprised to notice, since she had entered the café, but had since stopped. She saw something moving down the alley, amongst the wet cardboard boxes. It sniffed at them, causing them to fall, ran away, came back a few moments later and cautiously climbed inside one of the boxes. It was definitely a fox; the tail gave it away. Zoe peered carefully to see what would happen next. *Were there more? Was it attacking something – a cat, perhaps? It must be injured if it didn't jump from the boxes as they fell to the floor… Do foxes attack cats, anyway?*

With a loud clatter, the thought was broken. Zoe spun her attention in surprise back to the table. The waiter had returned and placed a cup and saucer vaguely in front of her, clumsily and without raising his eyes from the coffee. He grunted an unconvincing gratitude and then left as suddenly as he had arrived, working his way from booth to booth, from raised arm to raised arm.

Zoe half-stared at him. She had completely forgotten about the graffiti.

Slowly, she lifted the ashtray with her left hand and returned it again to the exact centre of the table. In her right hand, her cigarette had burned away to nothing. She scooped the cold ash and tossed it casually under the table, reached into a side compartment of her bag for a tissue, wiped her hands and lit another cigarette. She shook the packet. Less than half empty. She dropped it onto the table and then filled the holder with the few remaining cigarettes.

The clock on the wall was slightly crooked.

Its heat-warped, plastic hands never quite managed to settle on the numbers which they circled every hour. The time it currently told was twelve thirty-five, or as close as the clock could ever be expected to *get* to twelve thirty-five. Its grease-stained face was the exact sort of thing which Zoe felt the world was turning into. And there was nowhere you could turn to escape it; the clocks, the

34

awkward seats, the tables, the dustbins. The covers of the books at work.

Everywhere was plastic, everything was disposable.

In another age, she would be sitting in a coffee house, she thought to herself. She would be sat on a solid oak chair at a solid oak table. Maybe music would be playing discreetly. Nobody would be bothering anyone, nobody would be staring at her all of the time in places like *here*, she thought, almost aloud, as her eyes scanned the oblivious room with a new disappointment.

People were more *relaxed* back then, whenever it was. She wasn't too sure and was too tired to think, but she knew there'd *been* a time like that.

She knew those places still existed, though. Places where the clocks strike a timeless chime every hour as the large hand falls exactly between the X and the II. Where the furniture is of a quality that you would never even *think* of defacing with cheap library pens.

Zoe looked at her hands and sighed. They reminded her of those bloody library books. Without lifting them to her face, she could *taste* their smell. The smell of the houses of the teenagers who Zoe could not bring herself to even *look* at, who would take out the 'Nobody Understands Me' novels time and time again because they thought they could see themselves in the characters. They would smell of the bungalows of those smug, self-centred, self-righteous little old ladies and their large-print love stories, and their bitchy comments about Zoe's bangles and skirts. They would smell of the musty yellowed pages of the twenty-year-old hardbacks covered in transparent plastic that contained pathetic yarns of distant galaxies, predictable maniacs or espionage.

She finally raised her hands and sniffed them, and suddenly it took every ounce of strength she could find to not scream and cry.

"What's the point?" she heard the words inside her head like an old mantra, "Oh *God*...what's the bloody *point*?"

What is the point of lying to *yourself*? Finding a career just to convince yourself that that is what you *are*, just so that you can say you are *something*?

She knew this day would come. She had known it, really, all along. The day she'd finally admit to herself how lost she really was. She just wasn't expecting it to be here, and now.

Zoe rubbed her hands together, as if doing so would make the stench of the books go away. She reached for the half-forgotten, half-cold cup of coffee and took several small sips in quick succession.

She screwed her eyes together tightly and then glanced around the room quickly to see if anyone had been watching her. Nobody had.

She stared hard at the clock. It was 1 am.

Zoe felt tired.

The day had sped by.

The thought of returning home to bed now cheered Zoe up. It was well before 2 am, and this made her feel somehow guilty for feeling tired so 'early' as if she were betraying herself. But this feeling lasted no more than a couple of seconds. Feeling tired and

36

with her hands wrapped securely around an overlarge cup, Zoe had thought of something about the library that she liked. That she actually *loved*.

Zoe had thought of Frank.

A new mood had filled her; a mood that she would forget even existed whenever it wasn't present. But when it was present: it flooded her. A mood that, when it came, Zoe liked to think of as actual happiness.

Frank was a regular visitor to the library. On the first Tuesday afternoon of every month, he would return six books to the library between the hours of two and three. His tastes were varied, yet not impossibly so. After scrutinising the shelves for a full five minutes at least, he would take six more books and place them on the counter, library card in hand. None of that fumbling through wallet compartments and deep pockets that you get with other customers. And he always said: 'Thank you', Zoe had noticed, in a genuine way. No one else *ever* said: 'Thank you'; like they meant it, she'd thought. A 'Thank you' for scanning their boring book, a 'bless you' when they hear you sneeze; nobody else ever *really* means any of it.

Zoe prided herself on the fact that she had never thanked *anyone* for over a year. Not when they handed her their library card, not when they put their damn books through the barcode machine. Why *should* she? What was she supposed to be thanking them *for*? If anything, *they* should be the ones thanking *her*, she believed, if they wanted the bloody books so much.

But Frank? He *always* said it. Every single time. Never to Zoe, though.

Zoe could never bring herself to serve him. Every time she tried, her stomach would turn and her heart would feel as if it were stuck in her throat. She would always suddenly find other work to do; papers would suddenly need filing, or paper clips in a faraway office would suddenly need to be tipped out of their boxes and put back in again. Something, *anything* would need doing that was more important than serving him.

Zoe pressed the cup to her cheek. The coffee was too cold to drink now, but it didn't matter. It cheered her to think that thinking of Frank had distracted her so much that she forgot she was in the middle of drinking it. It *must* be love, she thought.

How else could she possibly get so distracted? She smiled to herself as she dwelt on the idea. She inhaled deeply again through her nose,

but this time with contentment, and her smile grew wider.

From nowhere, Zoe suddenly felt so excited that it took every ounce of self-control she had to stop herself from screaming, this time with joy. She wriggled in her seat to contain her excitement. The action reminded her of Christmas Eve when she was a little girl; all of that barely containable elation that had no alternative than to be realised without a trace of a let-down was here *again. Maybe she was no longer lost, no longer alone. Maybe this was...it. After so many years of waiting maybe it was finally here. Real Love*, she thought to herself.

Real Love. Capital R, Capital L. The real thing.

Zoe placed the cup back onto the table and began to absent-mindedly drag the ashtray to the centre of the table with her finger, and spin it on its axis.

Frank and Zoe. Zoe and Frank. She repeated their names over and over to herself in her mind as the ashtray slowly span. How right they sounded together as if neither name could be replaced with another. It could be nothing short of destiny.

Destiny. The word triggered a thought in her mind.

There was a time, some eighteen months earlier, when Zoe had booked herself a train journey to London, for no other reason than she needed to be alone and far away from everything she knew. Zoe would constantly mention the trip in deliberately

constructed conversations with Jenny Reed at the library, casually letting the subject arise. The whole idea had started as a lie at first, an ice-breaking, eager-to-impress fantasy, and after the conversations were over, Zoe would curse herself for starting them.

It was on Zoe's slow journey home from a lonely night in a London hotel that this act of 'certain destiny' had taken place.

Walking fast through the centre of the city, she became aware of the shape of a familiar figure in the sprawling crowd in front of her, and her quick steps stopped instantly as her whole body froze. It was Frank. Staring into a clothes shop window.

Zoe didn't know what to do. *Why is he here? Out of everyone?* She thought, and her heart raced with fairy-tale delight as she wondered about the possibility that he might have followed her down to London. She scurried through her bag for her phone and frantically pretended to be calling someone, not daring to lift her head and not knowing whether to walk fast or stand still as her heart raced and her hands trembled.

39

The moment felt like a million movies Zoe had seen, of romantic scenes that she had spent a lifetime mocking but secretly longing for. Taking a gulp of air she squinted, looked ahead and froze again. He was walking straight towards her.

Memories of Frank flashed through her mind as she stood there – thrilling little images that made Zoe's whole body quiver and she felt her empty stomach churn. She briefly recalled how she once plucked up the courage to replace books on the shelf near where he was standing. She felt the same quick thrill right now as the time she had waited for him to be served and leave the library before subtly noticing his card and learning his name from it. She had wanted this, or something like it, or indeed *anything at all* to happen all of her life and now here it was. Here of all places; *here it was*. The enormity of the occasion began to hit Zoe at full force, and she felt a rush of panic fill her chest. Then, just as Zoe finally began to raise her head, to let him see her standing right there in front of him, she instinctively shot her gaze back to the floor and rummaged through her bag, and the world began its familiar feeling of falling from underneath her.

Those few seconds he took to walk past her felt like the longest of her life. With every step, she cursed herself for staring at the pavement again, but still, she couldn't raise her head. It wouldn't budge. She was helpless. Then, holding her breath tightly and feeling as if she were tensing every possible muscle from her neck up to do it, she raised her head gently.

It was too late. By the time her head was raised again, Frank had gone. A crowd had replaced where he should be standing.

Zoe felt empty. She began walking quickly as her chest pounded and converted her panting stare into a casual glance at the nearest shop window. She couldn't turn around. She knew the reason why; in case Frank wasn't running back to tap her on the shoulder. But she couldn't admit this to herself. Nevertheless, amongst it all, she felt happy for seeing him. Then delighted. And then, almost drunk on the adrenaline of it all. *Here of all places! Today of all days! And so far from the library!* All of this could not be ignored in Zoe's mind. Frank had probably been too nervous to speak. That's what it was. *Obviously.*

She smiled all the way back home from that moment; through every cold mile of the train journey, all the way back until three thirty-two the next morning when she finally went to sleep again in her own bed. By this time, she had convinced herself that what she had experienced that day was too unlikely, too real yet unreal, too…*non-coincidental* to be a coincidence. This was bigger than chance. It was, she was overwhelmed to announce with her final words before sleep at last arrived – Destiny. *Capital D.*

The joy of this oft-remembered tale ended as she recounted the last moments of it in her memory. Suddenly, in the time it took her to blink, her small smile dropped. Zoe stared, glazed, dead ahead at the blackened café wall. She realised it, now. Frank didn't love her. *Forget it.*

She could feel tears welling instantly in her eyes and she gave a large, uncontrollable shiver. How could he possibly *love* her? He had seen her once a month for around an hour at a time over the best part of seven years and never said so much as *one word* to her. Not once had he smiled first. Christ, and the time in London. That was nothing different to the couple of times she had seen him around their local town and she had done exactly the same thing. So, he was in London. *So bloody what?* Travel was more common for normal people than it was for her, she thought to herself. She could've probably raised her stupid head and seen *dozens* of people she knew there.

The speed at which this thought came and secured itself amazed her. She tensed every muscle in her entire body. *Stupid bitch,* she heard her mind scream.

Zoe stayed staring forward. The front of her head felt heavy as if it were drooping over her eyes, and she thought about the fluff-coated painkillers in her bag, and how they never bloody worked anyway. She thought about what a fool she had been making of herself for the last seven years, every day and every night. *Just another senseless infatuation. Just another distraction from life.*

Love was a four-letter word, Zoe thought. Love was *several* four-letter words. Zoe cursed Frank in whispers as her eyes filled with tears which refused to fall. She really could've Cared about Frank.

They really could've Got To Know Each Other, really Know Each Other's Every Thought and every other wishful cliché that everyone else seemed to find so naturally. But Frank was not interested.

42

Clearly. Christ, he probably didn't know she even *existed*, either. It was those clothes, she decided. It was those stupid bloody blouses, those stupid bloody skirts and plastic beads. Frank probably hadn't got the bloody intelligence to look beyond the surface, anyway. *Stupid idiot. Another fake. No one* can *possibly* read six books every single month, she thought. Frank probably didn't. He was probably some sad little man desperate to impress, wanting strangers to believe he was well-read. How tragic can one person be, she thought, trying to impress strangers who aren't even looking?

Zoe broke her flurry of resentments to blink her eyes hard in an attempt to rid herself of those frozen tears. As her eyes cleared, she noticed she was staring at a man in the booth facing hers. She recognised him.

He lived in her street, at the opposite end. A man she once felt she loved. Long ago. They used to speak to each evening as she returned home from work. But not now. Not since she had seen a stranger, a woman, getting into his car one evening when Zoe returned at the exact time she knew she could collide with him. They kissed and drove away. The bastard.

From that night, she always walked home down the opposite end of the street. This made more sense, anyway, she would tell herself; it was nearer to her flat, and was nowhere near as terrifying a journey. Under the railway bridge, everything was pitch black and damp. She referred to her old route as passing down the 'Dead' side of the street. And lately, she had started to feel as though that side of the street was growing a little darker, a little bigger, and a little closer to her door, every time she left her home.

The man and Zoe looked away from each other at the same time. Zoe looked back to the table beneath her. It was blurred and distorted through her wet eyes. She opened her mouth and stretched her facial muscles lengthways, and her eyes ached. Raising her eyebrows she uncontrollably emitted a sharp, loud sigh that sounded as if she had just learned of some half-expected dreadful news. She repeated the noise. Slowly, after wiping her face, she rested her head on her clenched fists. Zoe stared vacantly at the empty seat facing her for a full half-minute, thinking of nothing, of no one, not even herself. Not one single, solitary thought arose in her distant mind. Then, in one sudden, rapid movement, she swept all of her belongings into her handbag.

Zoe stood bolt upright. For a few seconds, everything looked black, as if she were blind. She gasped, as she always did when this happened. *Not hungry though*, she thought aloud, as if answering some invisible, nagging parent. She leant on the table with the flat fingers of one hand to stop herself from falling over and waited for the terrible sensation of light-headedness to pass. Slowly, she steered her head to where she knew the clock was hanging and waited for her vision to return. It slowly returned. The clock said the time was sort of one forty-five.

Dropping the correct change for the coffee onto the table with an embarrassing thud that she didn't even hear, Zoe tugged at the long strap on her handbag as it hung over her shoulder and walked hastily to the door. Almost fully recovered, and still thinking of nothing, her wet eyes darted around the room for the final time. Her actions of the last few minutes suddenly seemed incredibly loud and obvious in her mind. But no one even glanced in her direction as she left the café for the final time.

The cold early air and the smell left by the rain engulfed her. For a split second, she thought it would knock her off balance, but she continued walking.

The wind was howling around her head and, it felt, inside it. Cold raindrops occasionally flicked her skin as she shut her eyes against their sting. She felt the wind take her breath away and felt powerless to fill her lungs again.

Looking across the street, she saw two taxis parked and waiting. She thought about the money in her purse and assured herself she could easily afford one before deliberately walking past them at top speed, cursing herself audibly as she did so.

As she passed a street light, she wondered again what time it was, not wanting to look at her watch. It must be around two by now, she decided. She *couldn't* look at the watch.

All she did at work all day was look at that bloody watch. She used to love it. She had longed to buy it and did so with her first week's wages from the library. Now she loathed it. It was a constant memory of the library. Even now, the only reason she wanted to know the time was to see how many hours she had left before having to return there.

Momentarily, she decided on forcing herself to stay awake, so that she could have a few more hours away from work without just slipping into the routine coma and waking up with a headache ready to do it all again. But the emotions of the evening were too overbearing. At whatever cost she had to get them out of her mind.

Zoe arrived at the safe end of her street twenty minutes later. She raised her head for the quickest of moments to glance along its length and width. It felt so much darker than any other street she had walked down that evening, she thought, as she blinked her cold eyes hard. It seemed there was a sullen, empty void that was hovering above head level. The street lights seemed to be glowing with a luminous blackness behind their yellow glow.

As she approached the gate to a garden which the residents shared and collectively ignored, she had confirmed again, just to be sure, that yes – she would go straight to sleep and that yes, she definitely despised Frank. This was no longer confusion speaking, if indeed it ever was. She decided she would treat him the same way as she did all the others. Everyone. The same way they treated her; no more effort. The dream was over, and for a distracting moment, it scared her how quickly she had flitted between love and hate for Frank. But only for a moment.

Zoe walked along the garden, returning to the gate to close it again after the wind had thrust it open. She gave it a couple of extra shoves to ensure it was shut tight. Walking to the door, she yawned and the cold wind blew inside her mouth.

The key fitted into the lock and the door thrust open as if it were being done for her. She closed the door as quietly as she could so as not to wake the neighbours. She was warming now, albeit slightly.

Zoe pressed the sleeves of her blouse to her arms, making her skin momentarily cold again.

Sliding the chain across the door, she walked up the flight of stairs to her apartment.

After a slight struggle, Zoe opened her apartment door. She thought about how *empty* her mind felt, how completely...*empty*. Closing the door behind her and locking it, she tried to remember what this feeling reminded her of. Then it struck her. It was the same kind of feeling she got after being thoroughly drunk during the day, yet sobering up almost completely in time for bed. Except this time she was aware, she believed, of absolutely everything she had said or done. And she was in no doubt of her decisions. They were correct, and as she had proven countless times before, she would be sticking to them.

It wasn't only the simulated drunkenness that was familiar, however. Zoe had recognised the feeling she had had before all this Frank business, a feeling she had known for all of her adult life.

She felt...*right*. Zoe felt empty, alone, numb, but *right*. The thought scared her, and her tears fell again as she pulled the bed sheets over her head.

The night was no different to any other. Not for Zoe. Not for anyone.

At the 'Dead' end of the street, underneath the damp cold bridge, amongst the shadows which were blacker than black, stood Frank. He was in more or less the same spot he had been in for the last hour. He watched Zoe's bedroom light through her pink cotton curtains until it shone no more. He stared at the blackness of her window for a few moments and blew a gentle, prayer-like kiss towards its closed, now-familiar shadow. He turned slowly and began walking home again, eyes fixed on the floor, tugging at the long leather strap on his bag, and without looking behind him.

A Spectacular Night
in the Dull Life
of the Man who
Didn't Exist

"It's not so much that the day has dragged," Paul replied into his mobile phone.

The rain had soaked the screen so much that he was scared to wipe it in case he suddenly exploded. A vision flitted through his mind, distracting him momentarily from the conversation, and an audible image formed of his sister's panicked voice on the end of the phone as it lay on the ground.

"Hello...hello, Paul? What was that noise? Paul are you ok?", he pictured her calling in a growing wave of words while his electrocuted, rain-soaked body lay twitching on the pavement, ignored by passing, and probably laughing, motorists.

The demise felt like it would be a fitting end. A suitable punctuation for the insane but predictable workday he had somehow survived. Paul smiled

49

slightly at the image of his peculiar death and began to smile even more gleefully when he realised that death would be a pretty watertight reason for not having to go back to work again tomorrow.

He blinked to break the alarmingly-comforting thought and decided that exploding wouldn't be a very good thing to do at all. He moved the phone slightly away from his cheek as if this action would secure his safety in a freak electrical catastrophe.

"You still there? Emily? Em?" Paul asked. "I was saying the day hasn't just dragged, Sis," he sighed into the phone, "It's more like - if there was a sudden announcement on the news when I get home that NASA is sending a rocket straight at the sun, I'd say 'where's my seat'. I'd say, 'I don't mind standing if there are no chairs, just let me on'. I'd say, 'Tape me to the tip of it by my feet with a pole up my back so that I get to hit the sun 5ft 11 inches sooner than the rocket does'. So, it's not so much that it's dragged, Sis, no, it's kinda more like I hate everything about my life and was actually praying for alien abduction before I called you. Hello? Emily? I said I hate my life and it's raining. How are you?"

He waited for empathy, but none came. "What?" replied Emily in an irritated tone, as if distracted by a child rather than a man ten years older than her, "Sorry I was...did you say something about a rocket? Paul, I've not really got time for this darling, I'm going out in an hour, he's not even back from the pub yet, and I've lost my...ugh, why would anyone even move my bracelet? I hate these people; I swear to God I do. I loathe my family, Paul. Sorry sweetheart, what did you say about today? You saw a rocket? That must have been...well...fun for you, or something like that, I'm guessing?"

Paul stood still in the heavy rain, momentarily speechless. "I said...no, Emily, for God's sake, I didn't say that at all, I said...look it doesn't matter what I said. Today was ok. Ok? Same as every other day. Forget it. It's raining. Can you still pick me up? It's really raining."

Silence met his question. He took a moment to glance back down the street, suddenly feeling like the victims in a million crime reconstruction dramas he'd seen on TV. A strange noise in the phone startled him, and he began to instinctively walk sharply. "Emily?" he half-shouted into the device, with one wet finger in his free, dripping, ear, "Sis, Em, what's wrong?"

He pressed the phone closer to his ear as he quickened his pace. The line crackled before the reply came.

"On its side, for God's sake, Paul; my nail varnish was in a kitchen drawer of all places, on its side. Do these people know what nail polish does to wood? Why do they move my things, Paul? The lid was on so the drawer's ok, but oh my God, my knees are killing me. I actually think I'm stuck right now, Paul. Your sister is 35 years old, and she has no knees. How does this news make you feel?"

Paul rolled his eyes at the words, and heard a loud crack; the familiar sound of his sister's knees, as she rose to her feet.

"Ugh, there. Oh my God," she continued, "Sorry. What were you saying about the rocket? I worry about you, Paul. Are you still seeing your therapist? I need to call mine...I mean she's a wreck, but... hey

51

did you talk to that weird little woman at work yet? The tiny redhead with a sex drive instead of a personality? How's that all going, lover boy?"

Paul waved his arm in front of his face, exasperated as if clearing the air of the conversation. "Look, Emily can you still come and pick me up?", he repeated, "The rain is bouncing, I'm soaked, and you said you'd..."

"Aw, Paul I'm sorry," came the expected reply. "I'm going out and I'm not even half-ready yet, sweetie. And he's not back. He's sat in some pub with his friends, wearing their hats. I mean, ugh it's the hats that do it, you know... that's the thing out of all of it that pisses me off the most, I mean – you're indoors, for God's sake, wearing a hat, you know? He's a grown man, Paul, actually inside a warm room, wearing a hat. That's his new personality substitute now he's shaved the beard off. A Beanie hat. I'm like, are you seven? Is that it? Am I dating a seven-year-old, or something, is that it? Because frankly, I think he's about seven, emotionally, on some levels, at least, you know? What do you think, Paul, you've met him."

Paul stood still again, speechless. His eyes grew wide and his brain felt numb from the day, and this unexpected tirade of self-centred bullshit. He sighed. Deliberately and loud, so that she could hear. Then he wiped the phone screen dry with his sleeve and hung up.

"Fuck you, too, Emily," he said, looking at the now-blank screen. "Have a good night and fuck you too."

Paul glanced again down the length of the street. He saw nobody approaching and very few cars. He sighed, a sound he had heard himself make in a million mundane moments, and in the instant that he turned around, Paul's entire world changed, incredibly and forever.

On the pavement in front of him, some eight feet ahead and facing him, stood what Paul instantly and unavoidably recognised to be himself. In every detail.

The fact occurred to him as simply and bluntly as that. He didn't even have time to register the impossibility of the situation. He simply, impossibly, but very definitely saw himself, in every detail, standing in the very clothes he was wearing at that moment. Same black shoes, with identical scuff marks from the radiator next to his office desk which he constantly kicked whenever he crossed his legs. Red tie with identical ketchup stains worn at the same ragged, reluctant angle after a ragged, reluctant day in a job he despised. The same windswept, rain-soaked hair. An identical look of open-jawed surprise on his face. Paul froze and felt a wave of adrenaline flood his body.

There, standing in the rain, in the storm, in his jacket, even, stood Paul, staring back at himself. Both men simultaneously sighed a gasp of confused disbelief and took a single cautious but curious step towards each other.

"Who are you?" asked Paul, quite understandably.

"I don't want to sound obvious but who are you?" came the reply, "You... you look exactly like me!" he continued. The man's gaze alternated between wide-eyed bewilderment and furrow-browed scrutiny as he scanned Paul's face and clothes, registering each identical scuff and stain and wrinkle. The man's awkward giggle as he spoke reminded Paul of the sound he himself made; an involuntary mix of fear and shock. It was a sound Paul himself had made on the few times he had been aggressively confronted by strangers in the street, or asked to donate money for a colleague's birthday gift at work.

Paul wanted to say "No, you look exactly like me,", but didn't bother. He felt that opinion had already been established by the man standing in front of him. Not even slightly relaxing as time passed, he nevertheless stepped closer until they stood inches apart.

"I'm...Paul," stammered Paul, feeling as if he should explain himself.

"Hang on, I'm Paul," came the reply, with another furrow-browed gaze.

Paul stared back at the response, and both men began to scrutinise each other for confirmation of what was happening; the same grey shirt, supposed to be white but faded from a lifelong ignorance of washing machine instructions. More matching ketchup stains, this time around the third shirt button, from where he had been sitting, more or less on his back, in his office chair at lunchtime, spilling his sandwich. It was even smudged from where he had frantically tried to suck the sauce from his shirt when nobody in the office was looking.

"Is...is that...please tell me that stain is blood and not ketchup," the man said, nodding at a dotted red line on Paul's shirt.

To anyone else on earth, the sentence would have sounded ridiculous, nonsensical, or as a sign of some fractured mental state revealing itself. To Paul, it made total sense as the surprise further confirmed itself to him.

"From the cut when I missed my sandwich and bit my lip at work, yes," Paul replied as if to personalise the stain as he stared at the mirror in front of him.

The familiar stranger opened his mouth to speak, but Paul spoke first.

"Look I don't want to state the obvious here, and I think this is a reasonable question, but what the hell is going on?" he asked, staring the man in the eye, and gasping as he noticed a small scar at the top of his nose.

"Did...did you fall off a bike?" Paul asked, and the man automatically knew what the random words referred to.

"On the hill outside grandma's house when I was six," he replied with surprise, realising that he knew what the words referred to without explanation, "I fell over the handlebars because..."

"Because I hit a rock next to her patio and cracked my face on a rabbit hutch!" Paul said, completing the sentence in what felt like a statement more than a question, and touching his own identical scar.

"Yes!" gasped the man in a bewildered voice.

"No!" they both gasped simultaneously, as the bizarre truth started to register with them.

"How is this...what the hell is this?" Paul asked again.

"I don't know," replied the man immediately, "You say your name is..."

"I'm Paul," Paul repeated, "Paul Thornton."

"Paul Martin Thornton," replied the man, and Paul stepped back several paces at the revelation of the deliberately undisclosed middle name, "That's...that's my name."

The men stared at each other, both fully aware of the other's thoughts at this moment, but both equally aware of their own identity and the imposter standing before them.

The rain continued pouring, as the confused men stared at each other, both trying, somehow, to absorb the situation. Here, in front of them, stood themselves. Every stain, every confused facial twitch, every raindrop. Identical.

Paul did what instinct told him was the most appropriate course of action. Paul ran away. Screaming down the street he crossed the busy, rain-soaked road and on towards the fields at the edge of town. Turning occasionally, he saw the equally panic-stricken doppelganger racing after him, screaming something inaudible against the rain.

Paul dodged traffic as his sprint carried him further away from the scene. "What the hell is happening?" his fear allowed him to scream on three occasions, as he glanced back to see his terrified double dodging traffic as he followed behind.

From nowhere, Paul felt his knees buckle and then a thud as his head hit the muddy ground a fraction of a second later. He writhed on the floor and began clutching his head. "Christ!" he shouted in pain.

A few moments later, in a perfect repetition of his own fall, he turned to see his double fall over the same rock as Paul had, thudding his head in the small puddle that had formed in the dent left by Paul's fall. Both men screamed as their eyes met again.

This time, neither ran. Neither moved. They took the moment to begin scrutinising each other again.

"You're me," confirmed Paul.

"You're me," corrected the man.

"Look, let's not start all this again," said Paul, pointing a muddy finger at the familiar face opposite him, "It's not going to get us anywhere." He looked down at the mud that covered them both, "And neither of us is very good at running, clearly," he added.

In an automatic act of silent collaboration, both men helped each other to drag their bruised bodies to the shelter of a nearby oak tree, panting for breath as they did so. For a moment, they sat in silence, glancing at each other, and back along the street.

"Right," said Paul, in an attempt to convince himself he was gaining control of the situation. "We need to try and make sense of what's happening here."

"Oh, well deduced, Einstein," snapped the man sitting next to Paul in his clothes, and with his same sarcastic tone, "Let's do that, shall we? I was walking out of work to go and get my lunch, listening to my sister moan about her boyfriend on the phone and suddenly, bang, it's raining, it's night, and I'm sitting on the hill in the rain, after chasing myself down the street and nearly getting run over so yes," he confirmed, reaching the end of his enormous, angry breath, "yes; making sense of what the fuck is happening would be a really good idea, I agree."

"Hang on," said Paul, ignoring the familiar tone of the tirade as one he knew to be a fearful, scared rant, "Lunchtime...you said lunchtime,"

"Yes," came the reply from his identical companion, "One o'clock, lunchtime. And now it's night, all of a sudden. That never usually happens"

"What the..." stammered Paul as he comprehended the words and situation.

"And raining. I hate it when this happens, too," he said, pointing at the sky briefly, "How am I going to get my sandwich now? All the good ones will be gone by the time I get back. Oh, this is ridiculous."

Paul stared at the familiar stranger. His latest words hadn't registered yet. Something about his demeanour had distracted Paul to the point where the man's words had been a blur. There was a difference, Paul saw now. A pretty huge one at that, now that he'd noticed it.

Their clothes were identical, their rain-soaked hair and posture were like a mirror image of each other, and their facial expressions were like a reflection of despair.

Except, it wasn't despair that Paul now saw in this mirror-man. It was frustration. Frustration as if he had to be somewhere. The fear of exactly what was happening was responsible for Paul's frightened expression. But on the face of the man next to him, it was replaced, seemingly, with the visible frustration of a very inconvenienced man who just wanted his sandwich. Paul frowned at the realisation and the man's words finally dawned on him.

"Did...did you say...you hate it when this happens?" Paul stammered again, nodding his head slightly for confirmation or denial.

"Yes," drawled the man in a mock tone, as if Paul's question were the most stupid he had ever heard. "I'm never ready when it happens, and then, no offence, I have to go chasing some absolute lunatic like you...albeit a very good-looking one," he added with a grin at his living reflection, "to explain what's happening, so I can get back home. Sometime before the lunchtime rush at the café, ideally."

"Hang on, hang on," said Paul in genuine bewilderment, "it might be a really good idea at this point to tell me what the hell you're talking about. What do you mean, 'hate it when this happens', when what happens?"

"This!" shouted his double, with a frustrated wave of his hand through the rain.

"This what?!" shouted Paul back with the same frustrated wave.

"The dimension jump thingy!" exclaimed the man, with the exasperation of a professor reminding a child what 2 + 2 is, "And look, I'm sorry for all the insults earlier. I didn't mean it. It's just that in all this time, I've never met one with the same shirt stains as me, and never one with the exact same name! Oh, they're never going to believe this at work, I should get a photo."

The two men stared at each other as the rain lashed harder and lightning tore the sky above them. Paul's imposter nodded as he watched the words resonate around Paul's head, or so he thought.

"What the hell are you talking about?" Paul screamed again, rising to his knees in annoyed confusion, as the man frustratedly mirrored the move.

"The dimension jump!" repeated Paul's double, attempting not to sound too patronising as he

stated what felt to him like the obvious, "The jump in the dimensions...look I don't mean to be insulting but can we just sort this out, please? I've got a sister who's waiting to moan about me and a sandwich to buy."

"That's my sister moaning!" shouted Paul, automatically feeling defensive before remembering what he was talking about, "and what the hell is a 'dimension jump'?"

The mirroring ended as the man stared at Paul, his frantic, shaking frame looking genuinely fearful at what was happening.

"Oh dear," said the man, calmly. Paul suddenly sobbed in confusion.

"Is...is this your first time?" said the man, in a tone with a calmness that Paul had never seen before in himself.

"First time for what?" asked Paul, his whole face furrowing in confusion while the man remained in control.

"Jumping," asked the man calmly, recognising the rookie version of himself stood before him.

"What's...what's jumping?" asked Paul, his eyes scanning back to the route of their chase until they settled on the bridge near the scene of the fateful meeting a moment ago.

The man sighed, with the empathic professionalism of a police officer at the door of a family delivering bad news.

"It's called 'jumping'", he explained, "At least, that's what we call it in our bit of the galaxy." He paused the explanation there, as was customary, to let the news sink in, and his eyes followed Paul's, back to the bridge above the top of the road.

Laughter broke his gaze as Paul lunged forward, head and hands flailing in amusement, "Oh I tell you what," he spluttered, "I don't know who you are or who told you to do this, but you've got a bloody good sense of humour, I'll give you that." The man frowned slightly as Paul's laughing face scanned his for any sign of laughter. None came.

"It's always weird to hear at first, I know," said the man calmly, his face deliberately not mimicking Paul's. "There's a long version and a short version, but the upshot of both is: I'm you from another universe." He paused again to let the news sink in. Paul threw his head back in laughter again, harder.

"Oh, that's a good one!" he bellowed, pacing through the mud and scanning the nearby trees with his eyes, "Where are they, then?"

"Where's what?" replied the man in confusion, rising to his feet and looking at his phone, "Look, we haven't got time for this."

"Where are the cameras?" asked Paul, circling the nearby trees, "This is for YouTube, is it?" Is this for a tv show? Is your mask latex?" he asked, laughing, as he darted from tree to tree.

"No, Paul, there's no cameras. Look, we really need to get..."

"Did my sister put you up to this?" asked Paul as he continued his hunt. Thoroughly annoyed at the prank, he tried to maintain a fixed, fake smile, so that the viewers he pictured tuning in would not see his true, annoyed reaction.

"Paul!" shouted the man in a clearly annoyed tone. Paul froze again and his smile dropped as he walked towards the voice. "There are no cameras and it's not a joke, ok?" the man continued. Paul began to walk slowly toward the man, whose demeanour now told Paul that he really wasn't joking at all.

"Look, this isn't going to be nice or easy to listen to," said the man, as he had heard himself say many times before. "And don't have a go at me, ok? I know you, Paul. You have to trust me that I know you exactly as well as you know yourself."

Paul's catastrophic thoughts came to their conclusion. "Am I...am I dead?" he asked.

"You're not dead," sighed the man, who had been hoping the question wasn't going to come up.

"Oh God, no," cried Paul, ignoring the reply and beginning to spin and wail, "I'm dead, oh my God, why, why, WHY!" he screamed.

The man looked around nervously, "Bloody hell Paul, shut up, you're not dead. If you were I wouldn't be here would I. Look I don't know about our life on your timeline but on mine, it's a bit weird to stand in a forest screaming that you're dead in the rain late at night. Or any time, really. You might want to stop that", he added, looking awkwardly around for passers-by.

Paul became instantly silent as his thoughts continued to scream, and a questioning look fell over his face again.

"Then...then what am I?" he asked the man, weakly pointing at his chest.

The main rolled his eyes in a way Paul knew meant he was about to state the obvious.

"You're you", he said, confusingly.

"Look, I'll give you the short version since you seem a bit..." his eyes and face screwed up tightly as he assessed Paul's quivering, confused frame. "Nervy," he concluded his sentence.

"You're not special, ok?" said the man, flatly, as Paul frowned again. "I mean, yeah, you're special, you're a unique collection of atoms and all of that, ugh, ok you're special. You're special! okay? But the point is, you're not that special."

The rain prevented the scene from briefly falling into complete silence as Paul wondered momentarily why his entire existence was now being called into doubt. "What?" he decided to ask, instead.

"So...you know the universe?" said the man as patiently as he could, pointing at the sky but looking at his phone again for the third time, "Well, there are billions of 'em. Universes. And what it is, you see, sometimes they collide. They overlap. Only for a little bit, while they're flying around, and then it's all okay again."

"Hang on," said Paul.

"No," said the man, quickly. "Not got time to hang on. Anyway, we get it a lot where I'm from, out on the current far edges of infinity. Here towards the...primitive bit..." he glanced around in vague disgust, "Not so much..." Paul looked even more confused as the doppelganger continued.

"And what happens is...I mean they teach this in school in most universes, y'know... I mean there are an infinite number of child versions of us out there that know this, you idiot... but since they clearly don't teach you anything important here..... what happens is, basically, when the universes collide, and we all bang into each other, it only takes a storm or a bolt of lightning or a simultaneous sneeze and BANG!" he said, clapping his hands between their faces, "If we're in a similar place doing a similar thing when it happens...before you know it, this happens. I'm standing here with a 'me' like 'you', we're having this conversation, you're finding out how insignificant you are, and I'm going to miss my sandwich and get told off for being late again."

Paul felt his mouth fall open as he shook his head to try and make the words make sense. The man, him, didn't seem to be lying. He seemed, as far as Paul could read his own face, to believe every word he was saying.

"Millions of me?" he asked.

"Of us, clarified his double, "But yes; millions of you. Us."

"And...this happens all the time?" Paul asked, his eyes peering up, trying to find the infinite sky beyond the falling darts of rain.

"Always, yeah," said the man looking bored and glancing up at the sky with Paul. "Like I say, in most universes they warn you it's going to happen. Yours is a bit..."

"A bit what?" said Paul, dropping his gaze and looking momentarily hurt.

"A bit slow at this sort of thing," explained the man with a pitiful look on his face.

"Slow?" said Paul, now feeling defensive of a universe that he didn't particularly like from his own experiences, and feeling that calling it 'stupid' was a bit much. "Now, look..."

"We don't have time for all of this," Paul's distant twin said, his eyes darting at his phone again. We've got to get back up the hill. We've got about ten minutes."

"Ten minutes for what?" said Paul, his eyes gazing back up the hill to the bridge.

"The portal opened up there," said the man, with a stern look in his eye. It's going to be closed again forever in about ten minutes. I need to get back up there, get through it, and get back home. Ok? God, I hate this bit most of all", he said, rolling his eyes. "It's always a rush, it always gives me a headache, and I'm not even going to feel hungry by the end of it, so I can forget that sandwich." He sighed.

"Anyway," he sighed again, He began to run back towards the bridge without waiting for Paul's agreement.

"Why have I got to come?" pleaded Paul, looking at the journey ahead of him down the muddy hill and across the rain-soaked road. The man stopped, halfway down the hill, close enough for Paul to hear him, but shouting anyway.

"Because if I don't get back," he replied, "we stop existing. You can't have two of anybody in the same universe. The timelines permanently overlap, and we end up being erased from history. And you need to show me where we met. Right now. So move". He stared at Paul with pleading eyes, and Paul began to run with him.

The pair dodged the traffic, causing drivers to doubt their sanity at the sight of two average but entirely identical men moving in precise symmetry between the vehicles and across the grass verges.

Paul struggled to keep up with the man as they raced back up the hill and towards the scene of Paul's phone call with his sister.

"Keep up!" shouted the man in front of Paul. Paul, sprinting faster than any time since his childhood, watched the man's desperate run with a look of disgust on his face, "Do I look like that when I run?"

he wondered to himself and deliberately tried to streamline his position to make it different from the awkward sight running ahead of him.

Suddenly, Paul saw the man stop dead in his tracks, almost as if he were stopping himself from

falling off the edge of a cliff. He took a delicate step back and turned his head to look at Paul. Catching Paul's gaze, he stepped aside to reveal a small, glowing blue light. No bigger than a tennis ball, the light hummed as it hovered at waist height, and Paul similarly froze on the spot.

"The portal," explained the man, smiling. "See? Sorry for all the weirdness back there. And chasing you. I hate having to chase us. But like I said, not your fault if your universe isn't clued up on this kind of thing, is it?"

"I...I suppose not..." stammered Paul, his brain desperately fumbling for questions in exactly the same way he always knew it would if a UFO landed on the street in front of him.

"Can I ask something?" he exclaimed suddenly, conscious of the once-in-a-lifetime opportunity passing him by.

The man rolled his eyes in familiarity at the words, "Here we go again," he sighed, "About what?" he asked, briefly drawing his hand away from the portal. "Go on, about what?" he asked again, almost sounding frustrated at the enquiry.

"Well..." said Paul, unsure how to narrow his myriad of thoughts down into one question.

"Are you going to ask me if you're rich?" the man asked Paul with a smile. "Are you going to ask me if you're the boss of the company or just another number on the payroll sheet like here? Or maybe you're going to ask me if she *loves* you," he emphasised the word, knowing it would grab Paul's attention. Paul looked up with pleading eyes.

"Ah, there we go," grinned his double. "It's always one of those three. It's the job or the money or the woman. You never want to know how your health is, you know? You never want to know if you're sane. If you're happy. Well here's the thing", said the man, removing his hand from his pocket again for a final check of the time.

"You're all of those things. Okay? All of them. You're a loved-up multi-millionaire who owns two islands. And you're the homeless, illiterate pauper she'll never look at. You're everything in all of those universes. Some of them are happier than you, and some of them are a lot more miserable, believe it or not, and for really good reasons. And we're all you. But you're the only you in this universe.

"So it doesn't mean this is your role in this one," the man concluded, pointing again at the stains on their ties, and their dull, worn-out shoes, "It doesn't mean that this version of you is all you're ever going to be, or all you ever can be. Get the job, get the money, and tell the woman you love her. That's what I did."

Paul's jaw dropped again at the words, and both men glanced at the portal as it let out a static crackle and shrunk slightly.

"That's what...you did?" asked Paul, stepping closer.

"Yep," smiled the man, laughing suddenly, "I've got everything you wanted, by the looks of it. I did everything you're scared to do, Paul, I said everything you're scared to say". He glanced at Paul's clothes again, "To be honest, I'm only dressed like a mess today because we're decorating the new office at work. I don't normally look like this," he said, scornfully flipping his tie and pointing at Paul's grubby, well-worn clothes.

"Anyway", he added with a smug grin, "Good luck with… whatever mess your life is in, Paul, it's been… pitiful to meet you," he laughed, and turned towards the portal.

Paul, somehow accepting the situation now on some inner level, had felt his jealousy grow as the man spoke. Now with these final, derisory parting words, he felt it swell into anger and rage. Ignoring his double's well-practiced motivational speech, Paul dived forward across the street, unsure of the consequences of his move or the desperate gamble that made him do it, and stuck his hand into the pulsing blue portal. He felt an invisible grip hold his forearm and begin to pull him.

"No," screamed the man, his futile grasp on Paul's waist sliding away at the sheer strength of the pull in the opposite direction.

Paul slid further into the portal as his double grabbed again at his waist, this time, securing his grip on the cheap belt that barely held his trousers up, causing Paul's phone to drop to the wet floor and reveal a beeping call from his sister.

Paul had time to turn and see the phone, and see the man desperately reaching his hand towards Paul's face. In the next nanosecond, both men went hurtling through the portal, which snapped shut behind them, and vanished as if it had never been there at all.

On the floor, the phone call instantly stopped and the ownerless device returned to its factory default settings as if Paul, in this universe at least, had never existed at all.

How (not) to
be a Ghost

(A cautionary tale
for the recently deceased)

The one thing Greg always said about being dead was: it's really cold.

I'm really not sure how much I'm supposed to be telling you, or what I'm not supposed to tell you. As part of your 'Welcome to the Afterlife' Wellbeing Package, I've been asked to write the friendly welcome letter to ease your transition from one life to the next. But that was a bad idea, to be honest. You've probably noticed by now that your 'Welcome to the Afterlife' pack hasn't eased a damn thing. Additionally, I'm too bored up here to try and sound friendly, and this isn't a university brochure.

I'm not sure what I'm supposed to write exactly, but I don't think I can really tell you what 'life' is like up here without telling you about what happened to Greg.

First though, I feel like it's only fair to tell you about Greg, and the main thing about Greg was: he wouldn't stop saying how cold he was.

He said it to the point where it got annoying, in fact. No matter what the subject, no matter what he was doing with his afterlife, that was what the conversation always came back to. How cold it is when you're dead. As if we didn't already know.

He was right, of course. No denying that. You'll feel it after a while. The constant coldness. In mortal terms, you could compare it to those winter Sunday mornings when the heating hasn't kicked in yet, so you've got fully dressed and maybe put your dressing gown back on top of your winter clothes. Maybe two sweaters, even. And a T-shirt underneath it all. It's that kind of cold when you're dead. But with the difference that you know the heating is never going to kick in again. No radiators here to make a satisfying 'whoosh' sound as hot water floods and fills them and thaws you out. For eternity, though. Which, as you've probably already heard on Earth, is a very long time.

So I don't meet many ghosts who aren't always a little bit grumpy, now I think about it. I don't blame them; who isn't grumpy when they're cold?

But it doesn't help with the whole stereotype of ghosts, of course. There's nothing worse than a miserable ghost, whether you're on this side of eternity or down there on Earth. We accept that seeing us is alarming enough, and that's fair enough. Understandable, even. We would have been the same when we were young and naïve, or 'alive', as it's more commonly called. You still don't even know you're immortal when you're alive, if I recall correctly, and most of us up here usually at least try not to look miserable while we're down there. Unless we're assigned to do a haunting, of course. Although personally I prefer to smile then, too. Much more effective. In general, as a ghost, you don't have a good reputation. Unlike those who opted for reincarnation, of course. Lucky sods.

The smug smile on the faces of those who opted for reincarnation on my arrival to the afterlife, honestly, I knew right then that I'd made the wrong decision. Wait until you see them and you'll know exactly what I mean. There they were, lining up, going back to the physical realm as bunnies or lions or birds or trees or people; basically, the first thing that popped into their head that would put them in regular contact with the sun. Meanwhile, we grey ghosts stood watching them, wondering why we'd suddenly all started shivering when we didn't own goose bumps anymore. I personally blame horror movies for making being a ghost look easy. But anyway. I digress. That day is as blurry in my memory now as the day of your birth is to you, though. But Greg was right about the cold. It is really cold.

The competition between those who choose reincarnation over being a ghost is pathetic, sometimes. Ego is a human thing, a vile, human thing and up here we're pretty delighted to be free of it. But for some, on arrival, it's still residually present. You see them getting into these debates over what they're going to reincarnate as, and why their particular choice is the best one, which one of them is going to get a longer mortal life than the rest when they return to earth. But they're all wrong. There is no guarantee. The sapling tree that could be a thousand years old might get broken by a football after one week. Those returning as lions in the jungle might get killed by a poacher. And the idiots who get carried away with the 'Oneness of the Universe' realisations you get filled with when you arrive here and say 'I'll be a fly, please', are always back the same day looking really stupid.

Sorry. Here I am, moaning away. I'm here to do a job, so I'll get on with it. I've been here a long time, so don't let my bitterness get to you.

I haven't introduced myself, but that's part of the fun for me, to be honest. I'm not going to. I get a thrill out of that, I really do. We've probably met, actually; that shadow out of the corner of your eye when you were washing up...remember that time that you definitely - no I mean definitely - put that thing on the living room table but it just vanished into thin air and turned up in a drawer weeks later? That was me. You're welcome. And have you ever noticed how that one floorboard only seems to creak whenever you're alone? Huh, isn't that weird? Scary, I imagine, when it happens. Again, you're welcome. Yes, that was probably me too. I do get around quite a bit. So, although we haven't officially met: hi again.

I used to get around a lot more than I do now. The first 400 years of being a ghost, maybe even 600 if you don't let the old ghosts make you cynical, are a blast. Just, oh, a constant laugh. Seriously.

All those things you think when you're alive...which bully from school you'd like to haunt if you were a ghost, which people you loved in life, and how to make them happy beyond their wildest wishes and dreams - you get to do all of that. No limit, no right or wrong, just - do what you want to do. And you do it

73

all, 24/7, 365, without noticing weeks, years and centuries passing by.

I've followed amazing people since I died and made sure life never hurts them. I've followed total strangers, just for the fun of it, and randomly given them a poltergeist for the rest of their lives. Really, I've done that, just because I was bored, just because I could, just for a bit of a change. I've made lives magical, I've made lives miserable. Just for the fun of it. Just because you can when you're a ghost. God, you can pretty much do what the hell you want.

But like anything in life, too much of a good thing gets boring in death, too. I got bored and I got slack. So here I am, whoever I am, or was, telling you about Greg. Because that's my job, now. I'm not allowed back down to Earth for a century or two.

It's my own fault. I moaned one too many times that I didn't receive a proper induction when I arrived here. A full earth fortnight, the induction lasts. Mine was only six days. I've no idea why. But because of my complaints, they've given me a job in Marketing. Imagine that. Nine hundred and ninety-six years of some of the most legendary and notorious haunting the world has ever seen, and they've stuck me in Marketing. The lack of respect they have for me here is phenomenal, it really is.

Look, don't let all of this put you off immortality, by the way. I'm honestly not trying to scare you with this; there are lots of good points to being a ghost. I've said that. And that's partly my remit for writing this, I think. To let you know when you first arrive here that there's nothing about death to

worry about. But my point is that it's only any fun for those first four or so hundred years, and then it gets 'okay', and now it's just plain old 'boring', and that's not me being negative.

The main point I should be making for you newbies to the spirit world is, I suppose: don't fool about. See, a lot has happened up here lately that's never happened before, ever, so I thought I should include some kind of "polite" warning, or something like that, about it all.

So anyway, here's what happened to Greg.

Greg fooled about and became the first soul in the history of humanity to receive a fate worse than death.

That's the short version.

Greg fooled about and death is even weirder than life, is another short version. But now I've put those out there, I don't think that either version would serve as a very welcoming statement without some background information.

I don't remember how Greg died. It was gruesome, I remember him moaning about that, but you tend to forget everyone's tragic tale of departing their mortal body. You forget your own, so it gets as boring as hearing how someone got a paper cut on their finger, or what dream they had. Or how cold they are.

Greg was a ghost who really didn't enjoy it. Any of it. He didn't want to make the loved ones he'd left behind happy for the rest of their days. He didn't get excited at the prospect of terrorizing the ex who broke his heart or the teachers who gave him bad grades.

But the one thing 'they' don't like around here like is a lazy ghost. And that's what Greg became. I mean, there are rules here, y'know? What's total freedom without a few rules? It's a waste of the 'universal force', apparently, and I still don't know what that is.

The upshot is that if you can't make good use of that force, they make you use it. They don't kill you or anything; they can't, you're dead. But they can assign you to someone. Like a Guardian Angel. If you mess that up, you get banished to The Realm. Greg's the only ghost I ever know who got sent to The Realm.

Guardian Angel. I hate that phrase. If you knew the spirits that get assigned to be your Guardian Angels on earth, honestly, you'd hate them too. It's always the Gregs of the immortal realm. It's never the ghosts who want to help you. It's seen as a punishment. You've got a few centuries to spare before the next stage of spiritual evolution but you waste it by sitting there moaning about how cold you are? They'll find you something to do. Guardian Angel is the equivalent of telling a lazy employee to grab a broom and look like they're busy. If you've got one of those things, sorry to break it to you but they're there as a punishment for being lazy, not because you're special.

As for The Realm, every spirit I've ever met seems to have a slightly different version of what it is, exactly. Without wanting to spoil all the surprises I can tell you, and I really don't mean to alarm you, but there's a death beyond death. It's a punishment, so I'm sure it won't happen to you. Probably. Maybe. But as punishments go, it's easily the worst there is. It's the worst thing there could be. Death Beyond Death, to give it its less-than-inviting name, is also known as Ultimate Death. The Realm. Lots of foreboding names like that. The death of the soul. That indestructible force you're carrying can be destroyed. I know. Horrible isn't it? I'll spare you the details, or the details of the rumours, but I do know it lasts for several agonising millennia and I really wouldn't be surprised if all of the rumours about it were right.

But like I said, don't worry about all of that on your first day. You'll be fine, probably. Maybe.

Greg had been assigned to a random child in New Jersey, who was grieving the loss of his parents in an incident that apparently mirrored Greg's own demise in some way. I think that's why they sent

him there; they usually give the apathetic ghosts a relatable mission to get them interested. The kid had been drawing pictures of angels, too, so in theory, it was a good, standard plan. Greg met with the kids' parents up here and had a chat about what would be a good way to communicate. They make you have those conversations. It's a good thing, really, or else there'd be no difference between the Guardian Angels and the Poltergeists, which is what the rest of us are. Sometimes.

Greg's presence served only to make matters worse, however, due to his persistent interfering with heating systems wherever the small boy went. But Greg endured. He worked as hard as he could for several weeks. Day and night, Greg would give the child encouraging little signs. He would slightly move the treasured photographs and objects that reminded him of his parents, or slightly waving the arm of a teddy bear that the child's mother had given him each time the boy's tears flowed and he called her name.

Until one day, unable to restrain his constant frustration at the temperature of New Jersey in winter, Greg let out a scream of: "Why is it so bloody cold everywhere?". The words, for reasons none of us are still quite sure of, caused Greg to become briefly visible to the startled child. The child in turn screamed back at Greg, and the traumatic, scarring scene ended when Greg's repeated screams of "Get me out of here!" were finally answered.

Instantly assigned to a second role, Greg found himself in the small, cosy, and permanently warm home of a 90-year-old English woman, who had recently lost her husband to natural causes. Here Greg began to finally enjoy his work. The tropical temperatures that the permanently cold pensioner maintained in the bungalow instantly gave Greg the first trace of pleasure he had experienced in the afterlife: permanent warmth. Greg, for the first time relishing the prospect of being a ghost and feeling that as punishments go this was actually quite a good one, began to take delight in his Guardian Angel role. He would telepathically advise on lottery numbers to allow the old lady a few little windfalls here and there; he would find the ever-vanishing television controller and place it in full view to save her a frustrating, arthritic search for it. Greg was the perfect Guardian Angel.

There was one rather significant problem, however. She could see him.

A key feature of being a Guardian Angel is that the human they're assigned to is never allowed to see them. I'm not sure of the exact reasons why. Probably has something to do with that universal force stuff they're always droning on about. But the point is, it messes things up. Again I'm not exactly sure how, probably because of my half-assed Induction. I'm good at being a ghost, but I can't quote the whole 'Afterlife Manual' to you, if you know what I mean.

Anyway. It turned out the old lady was from a long line of natural psychics. She'd seen her grandmother's Guardian Angel, so, I mean, poor Greg never stood a chance. The big reveal finally came one night as she was watching the television and casually asked him if he'd make her a cup of tea before the lottery results were announced. Greg screamed again, and of course, was instantly dragged from the scene.

Another decade or three ticked by and I don't know what exactly happens in the next stage of the afterlife, but I know they don't let you evolve past being a ghost unless you've done your bit, so to speak. For whatever reason, hauntings aren't an option. All of that type of fun/malevolence, depending on how you see it, is mandatory. And you can't go on to whatever it is we go next until you've done your fair share of that. I'm still waiting to find out where we go next. A lot of us have been here on and off for several hundred years now, and we still haven't heard a word about Heaven or Hell at all, so I don't know what's going on there. I try not to think about it too much, and I'm not sure who to ask.

Concerns for Greg were growing. He needed to be somewhere. People on Earth were literally crying out for a Guardian Angel. Here was one who didn't want to go unless the radiators were on when he got there.

Eventually, it was decided that the safest thing was to send Greg back to his family. In a watchful way. A standard 'guiding and steering them' type of assignment; nothing too extravagant, and nothing too tragic. Despite his protests against this, it was agreed by the Senior Spirits that he'd be less likely to moan about the temperature and less likely to mess things up if it meant being close to his family again. It's a pretty cynical approach but it gets the job done, I guess. The world got another Guardian Angel, the powers-that-be got their universal force stuff balanced or whatever it is they do, and we didn't have to listen to Greg moaning about eternity.

Greg arrived back home to find his parents crying. It's a standard scene for Guardian Angels at that first family invisible reunion. He settled in quicker than most do, though, and before long he was making sure that his parents and his sister got through their days and nights as best they could. He'd follow their routines at work and college and around the home. He'd make his sister's pencil case appear from wherever it was when she was running late for a lecture. He'd sit in the empty seat

they left for him on the sofa each evening. He'd wrap invisible arms around them tightly as they cried and wailed through the night, until he felt like they felt his touch, and their crying was replaced by sleep.

Eventually, time passed, as it does, and their lives ended, as all lives do. Greg watched as one by one, his elderly family arrived at the afterlife and chose the reincarnation queue, unaware of each other's existence, unaware of Greg's presence.

The sight saddened him. As a ghost, you're not supposed to get attached. On any level. Even with family. Especially with family, because the day comes when they get into that reincarnation queue without the slightest idea who you are, and it feels horrible. Equally, while you're down there busily haunting or helping, you can't get too full of hate when you haunt that bully...you can't get overly helpful with that relative who can't pay their bills. You're there to help and guide and that's it. I think that's why Greg was reluctant from day one to return to his family, but that's the problem with eternal free will; someone's always telling you what to do with it.

Greg took the sight harder than most, though. The moment his sister arrived. No longer a wide-eyed college student but a creaking, bent, gaunt old lady. Greg cried. Her decrepit frame straightened and grew youthful again as she stood amongst the queue of spirits eager for reincarnation and a new experience of earthly life, and Greg cried harder. He wanted to be with her. As an eagle, as a worm, as a king or a rock, he wanted to be with her.

That's when it happened.

He raced from the holding bay where Guardian Angels are temporarily held between assignments and raced to where she stood in the queue. She didn't have the slightest idea who he was but began excitedly talking to Greg and the spirits around her about her excitement at what animal she might return as. She'd decided on a bird, she told them. And in a warm country. Permanently warm.

And then, she was gone. Into the light, back to earth, to be born, and soar, and die.

That was when Greg started wailing.

As fast as I've ever seen a spirit fly, he darted down the reincarnation portal after her. I mean, you just don't do that. You can't do that, it's impossible. We'd heard spirits talk about it for centuries, of course. Whispers about trying to make a break for a better, warmer life, or something. Sometimes even planning to chase after a beloved pet or partner as they returned to their next incarnation. But you can't do that; unless you've been assigned a new existence, the portal doesn't

lead anywhere. If you run through it without an Earthly assignment, you just end up standing behind it, in front of a very stern Senior Spirit who rewards your efforts with some kind of punishment, such as being assigned to a derelict building for a century or something. And that is about as pointless a job as you can possibly have in this existence. You maybe get to scare the occasional lost hiker every decade or so, or maybe the odd YouTuber here and there trying to tell you how they've come in peace and want to film you, but otherwise, it's a lot of time with nothing to do. And very cold.

But Greg didn't appear on the other side.

Dozens of Senior Spirits manifested immediately, of course, hovering around the reincarnation portal. The Senior Spirits are the scariest things I've ever seen. It's ironic because they're really quite friendly and helpful on the rare times you speak to them. But even then you're aware that they control your soul's entire destiny, so you're always going to be a bit on edge around them, I suppose. And even at their friendliest and most accessible, they're the scariest sight I've seen. Fifty feet tall. Blacker than midnight. Their human-like shape is made up of thousands of trapped souls, dark souls. Evil souls. Thousands of mute, anguished faces, writhing in pain and silently screaming in eternal agony, pulsing and pushing their way into view, to the front of that blacker-than-night body, in a pointless bid to be heard, or freed.

It's how they make sure that the most evil spirits on earth don't return, you see. The Senior Spirits absorb them. They carry them and their silent torture for eternity, so that each time a soul on earth is corrupted by evil, they cannot return once they die. Which is all very noble and fantastic for everyone down on Earth, but you try staring at all that when you're having a conversation with your boss and see if it doesn't freak you out.

They appeared out of nowhere in the instant that Greg vanished. They spiralled and swooped and roared around the entrance, but Greg was nowhere to be seen.

Within a couple of minutes, other spirits began reporting back from Earth in sudden droves to say that Greg had arrived there. The air buzzed with hundreds of frantic reports of sightings of Greg wailing, moaning, and floating at high speeds through traffic and streets and buildings, over lakes, skies and hills. Basically looking like every fake ghost video online, and ruining our reputation in the process, and that really annoyed the Senior Spirits.

It's the same with the aliens, you know. The UFOs. They don't stand a chance of getting their cool new ships filmed by humans when they joyride across Earth's atmosphere anymore. That all ended with the internet and AI. Apparently, they find it quite disheartening to travel all that way to show off their ships, only to find some little human has made a

83

flashier, sleeker, faster one on his laptop and stolen all of their attention. Quite sad really. But it does serve them right for trying to show off.

Greg's time on Earth didn't last long, as usual. I really don't know where he thought he would be escaping to, or how long he'd escape for, and neither did Greg, probably. But within about an hour of his attempted departure from the afterlife, he was brought back up, screaming even louder than he was before he vanished, and that was that. Off to The Realm.

The ironic thing is that about an earth-week after Greg's banishment, his sister returned as a spirit. Sadly, the raven she had chosen to be reincarnated as wasn't the brightest bird in the nest when the eggs cracked open, and in the confusion of opening her eyes for the first time and realizing she was alive again, she tried to fly too soon, and instead plummeted to the earth some 30 metres below, with a slight thud and several critical cracks. She's somewhere else now, again. She keeps coming back every few weeks, oblivious to her previous arrivals, and excitedly declaring her wish to return as a bird each time. Give it a few weeks or months, and back she comes, after falling from another nest, or head-diving into another windscreen.

It's funny, really, when you're up here watching it, I mean I know I shouldn't laugh, but I do.

So, there you go. I'm not sure I've been much help. I've probably told you too much, or nothing useful, but that's not my fault. Again, the training up here is shocking, it really is.

Look, you'll be ok. Ok? Ok. Just remember that you only get one shot at the afterlife. So don't waste it.

For everything I've told you, it's basically just the same as on Earth, if I'm honest. It's the same basic rule for a happy time. The same whether you're above the stars or beneath them, I suppose: be yourself, good or bad, and try not to act like a dick whenever you get cold.

Users

Offline

"Well. *I* didn't see him steal it. For all I know, I lost it. I dropped it somewhere, I mean, God, the way those trains just *shake* you before they even…"

"Carla, stop sticking up for him", interrupted Carla's mother. "Your purse is here one minute, you said so yourself, and then it's gone, and *he's* just sitting there wagging his tail with bits of cotton in his mouth. You're allergic to dogs, you silly little sod. Come on, we can get rid of him right now." Hearing her mother's words, Carla jumped from her seat on the windowsill and ran to the dog. She started sneezing even before her newly tanned arms were thrown around its bulging body. "Aw, Mom, no, not Archie, he's a *good* boy. *He* wouldn't eat my wages, would ya, son?" The dog, laying almost flat on the floor, appeared to raise one eyebrow briefly but did nothing else to indicate any kind of understanding or reply. Carla sneezed, hard, and her itching nose made a small but significant creaking sound. Her mother, balancing the kitchen bin on the breakfast table while she flapped open a new bin bag, span her head around to face the sound with a look of mortal horror.

"Carla. Oi! Put that bloody dog down. Carla! Stop it! You should know better at your age. Think I'm following *you* around all week with inhalers and eye

86

drops and Christ knows what else, you've got another thing coming. It costs you a *fortune* in prescriptions every time you so much as *think* about that dog and you won't put the bloody thing down".

Carla's mother walked around the table, straightening all the chairs as she spoke. Carla watched her mother through big brown eyes that could not see due to what was now semi-constant sneezing. The dog, again, did precisely nothing as the woman's words followed the girl while she rose to her feet and began to walk across the kitchen.

"Pumping yourself full of chemicals 'cos you're too stupid to keep away from your allergies," the mother continued, "Well, don't come crying to me when he's eaten everything you bloody own and you've sneezed yourself inside out".

With this advice and in one swift motion, Carla's mother threw on her overcoat, swept up her keys, purse and bag, opened the back kitchen door, and stormed out to a job she hated.

Carla frowned at the door and then smiled at the dog that barely knew she existed. "Time for me to get ready, Archie-Baby", she almost squealed, before kissing the top of her dog's oblivious head, grabbing her phone, and skipping to the bathroom.

Carla.
Usernames: Free_Spirit#10658, Dog_Mommy25

Carla Porter was the kind of grown woman who still called herself a girl more often than she called herself a woman. Short of offline friends, Carla had, until recently, lived life from glass to glass, from date to date, from night to night. A guy in almost every bar and fifty more hopefuls in her daily DM's. All were ready to jump whenever she made their phones vibrate. All were eager to show understanding when she rain-checked them for a better offer. Her social life, including holidays, revolved around which guy or guys would be available, where they would be, which month, and would her mother be free to take care of the dog. Never short of her own money, Carla was simply always hungry for male attention. As such, and by way of an empowering rationale for her lifestyle, her new dating profile location simply showed a globe emoji, a galaxy emoji, and the words *'free spirit'*. This weighty phrase was one she lived by via the dumbed-down, teenage definition of *'have sex with whoever stares back and call it freedom'*.

Carla's seven social media accounts each existed behind strict padlocks, but for discretion rather than privacy. Each had no more than ten followers who varied from app to app. Her 'Friends' lists were essentially galleries of guys whose attention she had toyed with over the years. Each of her uploads featured Carla in various 'casual' poses. Her photos, for those invited, showed hundreds of beautiful ancient landmarks which she seemingly believed were improved by casual glances of her ass or the side of her breast. Each upload and story was always greeted instantly by dozens of approving heart emojis from dozens of DM hopefuls. On her four family-friendly profiles, for balance, she would post pictures of her recent achievements at work, or volunteering at the local Dog Shelter, or doing jobs around the home. All would be immediately met with thumbs of approval from family members, ex-boyfriends and, occasionally, old school friends.

Recently, Carla had found herself experiencing awkward attention more often than positive attention from guys offline as well as on it. Her constant nights at home and more sober choice of clothes in recent weeks had been interpreted by her mother as a welcome sign that Carla was: "finally growing out of that childish phase."

In reality, Carla had grown increasingly sick of trawling bars for new guys and awkwardly meeting old dates along the way whenever she tried. Single ones, married ones, boys, men; all seemed to reappear at the worst time. Male friends from childhood she'd never quite dated but who suddenly needed her help to mend their recently broken hearts would appear at times that she really didn't want to 'help'. Off-duty doormen, on-duty waiters, even barmaids and club girls from her needier times, would all unintentionally catch her eye long after their nights or days together were over. All met her glance with awkward smiles while their well-practiced hands and equally well-rehearsed smooth talk were being given to some other girl. Lately, Carla felt suffocated by her life wherever she went.

As her single friends and flings all inevitably fell into steady dates or marriage, Carla begrudgingly decided she too had to settle down, find a dating app, and replace her social media thirst pics and fuckboys for the more formal picture styles her friends had adopted when first officially swiping right for love.

Her new profile featured a more clean-cut image.

All uploads featured Carla self-consciously wearing sweaters or coats, accompanied by her oblivious and overweight dog for added homeliness. Her rehearsed smile, her obese pet and her choice of clothing for each image would, she was sure, give a clean-cut, intelligent, trustworthy vibe to any high-earning, fast-living, frequent flying, entrepreneur with permanent abs who may be scrolling the dating app.

Tonight, lucky with likes, unlucky in love and with her mother's rants ringing in her ears, Carla was preparing to meet her first match from the dating app, after spending three solid weeks swiping exclusively left on every man under 6ft 2in, over 35, or who she thought her friends wouldn't be attracted to. Tonight, a 25-year-old travelling musician called Felix who looked very tall and rather young in his pictures would be meeting her in roughly ninety minutes. She'd noticed his thumb emojis of approval pop up in her notifications within minutes each time she posted a picture on the dating app. After viewing his profile and reading his confusing attempt at a bio: '*musician, single, live alone but can't accom, I am 25*', Carla found no other information listed and only superficial similarities, like proximity and age.

Curiosity piqued, she began to hunt for the mysterious Felix on other social media sites and search engines. Here she found no new information other than the fact that his 'Friends' list was public, enormous, and seemed to largely consist of girls who attended a nearby school and college. His picture galleries were also public and mirrored those on his dating app profile, except for a few extra images which seemed to be charting the growth of his moustache.

Carla had frowned in envy on first seeing the list of genuinely teenage girls before her but reasoned that Felix's band must have a large local audience much younger than him. An audience that was around the age Carla *looked*, she thought, as she shakily reassured herself with a glance at her selfie camera.

On the other side of the city, while Carla showered and sang, a clock shaped like a plughole with a Union Jack sliding down it failed to tick.

Its owner, Felix Butler, whose father had recently paid some £70 for this commercial, plastic icon of anarchy, failed to notice. The reason that he failed to notice had nothing to do with the fact that, despite its price tag, the clock ticked about as loudly as a cricket in a hurricane, and everything to do with the fact that his recently dyed and spiked hair was not behaving as he'd imagined it would before he had it styled.

"Spike, dammit, you....oh, come on! Spike *up*!" the boy whimpered at his hair's reflection. His hands, clad in fake gold jewellery, frantically clapped shut on either side of a chunk of hair, almost as if he were bullying it into shape. "*Just stick up, come on, pleeease!*"

The bedroom walls on either side of him were covered in expensive, glossy posters, none of which he had purchased. They gleamed behind glass frames which were polished regularly, but never by Felix. Each poster spouted slogans such as 'Burn Hollywood Burn' over a scorched US flag, flaming dollar sign or electric guitar. Another declared 'Beam Me Up Before This Shithole Explodes' and featured a green alien flipping a peace sign and smoking, presumably, a joint.

Felix.
Usernames: InsertWittyNameHere, Anarchy4UK

Felix Butler was an idiot. Unlike everyone else around him, Felix himself was unaware of this fact, despite regular reminders in his daily life.

The expensive posters around his bedroom were lit by permanently pulsing neon strips hidden out of sight, which he always felt would impress a visitor, were he ever to have one. His online presence suggested that guests were a common occurrence in his large house. Social media posts of his rock star poses amongst neon-lit posters of his current music idols were a daily event for his young followers.

Each upload suggested a hedonistic life of non-stop music, parties, and creativity. Each picture would feature a guitar, casually propped against a wall or hanging around Felix's shirtless neck. Each post was greeted with heart emojis by dozens of girls and women, all oblivious to each other's existence behind Felix's 'Friends' list, and all eager to be the one to get to know this enigmatic, travelled genius. Which, of course, Felix Butler wasn't. Felix Butler was an idiot.

In reality, the guitars, like the lights and the posters (and the video game dolls that *never* appeared on camera), were a series of gifts to Felix from his affluent parents. The shiny instruments hung neatly on an elaborate display in his large bedroom, where his fantasy of being able to actually play them had been living out in his pictures, mind and insular world for around two years now.

His sweaty, failed attempts at dating had earned him the nickname 'Incel' among friends as well as those who teased him. Felix's evenings were filled exclusively with video games, social media, and a serious but undiagnosed addiction to pornography.

Like many born to wealthy parents who achieve nothing of significance themselves, he had happily followed their orders to not speak with the regional dialect of those around him. Instead he adopted their perceived 'correct pronunciation', along with the ignorant belief that these sounds made him superior to anyone he met with an accent.

To Felix, freedom and class meant money. In reality, this meant sponging off his parent's bank accounts.

Until recently, his small circle of friends had exclusively been girls. Those with little previous male contact who grew close to him thought of him as strange but harmless. His attempts to mimic or adopt the personas of long-dead rock stars were interpreted by them as Felix's own persona, quotes and wisdom. Those more familiar with guys online and off it saw none of this in him, and instead quite wisely saw him as just another idiot in their DMs. All were subjected to his neurotic rants about what idiots all of their other male friends were.

All of them saw him as a Plan C, someone to have on standby when their Plan A and Plan B guys were busy with another girl or their partners. Felix had, after recently faking a breakup with his latest fictitious girlfriend, messaged them all across every app, telling them what had happened, how he

93

needed to talk, and how only they understood him.

Each girl had recognised the message as the invite for sex that such a message always is. But each had politely found a way to decline the offer. Felix, in one of his traditional rejection-triggered outbursts, instantly sent them all a new message stating that he had now made up with this non-existent girlfriend of his, before swiftly bulk-blocking all of their numbers and turning off his phone for a full, unprecedented, twenty minutes.

The few male friends that Felix now surrounded himself with knew nothing of his dating app attempts, despite their own failures online and in life in general. This knowledge, combined with Felix's already-strong feelings of inferiority, meant that online he was careful never to show his face above the thin, wispy moustache he was so proud of.

His own interactions with the many dating apps he had downloaded and deleted over the last month had all been the failures he had predicted they would be. Each optimistic App Store install had consistently been steered by the same unique approach. After completing his profile, Felix would routinely set his search criteria to include every straight woman of every possible age within a ten-mile radius. Other than clicking 'Block' on every face or name he recognised, he would then click 'Like' on every image of a woman that appeared on his screen.

Felix maintained this silent attack on all local eligible women each time a new member appeared on his homepage. Eventually, after four weeks of constant searches and regular 30-minute 'Profile Boost' attempts funded, unknowingly, by his father, he received a solitary 'Like'. A picture of him holding his guitar and looking casually away from the camera whilst propped against his bedroom bin had garnered a single thumb of approval. With the ice officially broken, Felix messaged Carla to thank her for the compliment. Routine over, their first lengthy conversation began, albeit one that largely consisted of the word 'lol'.

Tonight, preparing for the date, Felix felt sick. He was aware, to intensely anxious levels, that this was the night he would finally meet a girl, a *woman*, in fact, and be the envy of all his friends whilst finally becoming their equal, and no longer being single.

Tonight was also, in an eventuality he had been predicting ever since the date was first arranged online, the one night of the week that Felix's hair was looking nothing like the way he hoped it would. As a result, Felix was whining like a child in his bedroom.

"I only want my bloody hair to stand up..." he whined, pleading with no one in particular, his voice and mannerisms growing further by the second from the anarchist he thought that everyone thought he was.

"That's all I'm asking for...Christ...*look* at it."

Behind him in the mirror's reflection, Felix's desperate eyes caught a glimpse of his Sid Vicious poster. They locked on the images' hair.

The poster had been stared at as much as the mirror in recent months. Everything Felix had decided it represented was everything Felix had decided he was. Deep down, Felix knew that every time he stared at it, he did so with the kinship and relatability of a penguin staring at a polar bear.

Lowering his knees slightly to get more of the picture into the mirror, he began his ninth attempt to emulate what he saw.

Ten seconds later and his motorcycle-booted foot stomped on the floor in frustration.

"Oh, *God...*" he whimpered again, turning away from the mirror, "I look like a dick."

His eyes fell on the clock.

Finally, after a couple of seconds staring at it, he noticed that not only was the clock already pointing to the exact minute he was supposed to be picking up the dog from the vet, but also that it had stopped ticking.

"Argh!" he shrieked, "The dog... I'm dead!" and without giving a further moment's thought as to where to position his spikes to make them look like he *hadn't* spiked them, he grabbed his second deliberately scuffed motorcycle boot, shoved it on, and climbed out of his bedroom window.

Below in the rain, a voice shouted up.

"Felix, get back in that window and use the stairs like a normal person," shouted Felix's father, returning home from work with immaculate timing. "Go on, pretend you're a normal human being for approximately thirty seconds of your silly little life, Felix, and use the stairs like a normal person of your age would, and get the *hell* inside that window – *now*".

The leather-clad boy froze, having barely stepped halfway through the window frame and onto the wall trellis.

"I've got the dog," Felix's father continued, wearily. "Thanks for that, Felix, by the way. Very bloody much. I ask you to do *one little thing*".

"I'm in a rush Dad! I've done the washing up," Felix shouted back, making no sense whatsoever and without turning his head to look at his father.

"I don't care about *rushes*, Felix," his father continued wearily, "I care about wall trellis. I care about my Creeping Ivy getting snapped and making my house look like some kind of haunted bloody homeless shelter."

The boy, an ashamed eye falling back on the Sid Vicious poster inside his room, replied,

"...yes, Dad. Sorry, Dad," but remained still for the lecture.

"I care about my dog being left sat in the vets for half an hour like some bloody wild animal, Felix, that's the type of thing I care about," the parent continued, ignoring the routine apology.

"I know Dad, I'm *sorry*, Dad," stammered the embarrassed boy in the rain again.

"Why do you *do* this, Felix? Why are you *like* this?" his father continued, his posture relaxing in the rain as he fell into his bored rant, "This is the third bloody time I've caught you doing this, and God knows you're not going to tell me how long you've *really* been climbing down there, are you? Well, *I'm* telling *you* that I'm sick of telling you, Ok? So get in the window, and get down the stairs. Like a human."

"I'm sorry, Dad," muttered the rebel without a clue.

"Too much Netflix, that's your trouble. They're only *acting*, you know."

"I know Dad, sorry Dad", Felix replied, head now bowed in shame from the 'fuck you' sneer of Sid.

"Where are you going, anyway?" said the boy's father, with a frown, pausing again by the front door.

"I've...got a date, Dad," came the reply.

His father frowned, looking genuinely puzzled by the news. "A *what?*" he asked, stepping back towards his car until Felix was fully in his view again.

"I've...I've got a date, Dad. I'm going on a date," replied Felix, genuinely struggling to climb inside the window without scuffing his boots any more than the deliberate scuffs he had put into them.

"Who with?" his father asked, again with a tone of utter, genuine disbelief.

"With a girl, Dad," Felix frowned with his reply.

"What, a *real* one"?

"Yes, Dad! Oh my God! Of course, she's real! What kind of a question is...she's a girl, Dad, a real girl who exists and everything. *Seriously?* You're asking me if... wow."

Felix's father shook his head slowly, with the same bewilderment as if Felix were a hovering UFO trying to clumsily bang its way through the window into his son's bedroom.

"What, and she's *met* you? This girl who really exists has *met* you?"

"Not yet Dad, that's why it's called a *date.*" Felix's father was too busy trying to process this revelation to detect his son's attempt at sarcasm.

"Yes but, what, she's *spoken* to you, has she? She *knows* you?" he asked further, for confirmation.

"Of course!" shouted Felix, starting to feel more than a little insulted, but, half-hanging out of the window, literally not being in a position to do anything about it.

"What, and she *still* wants to meet you?" his father asked, his surprise genuinely increasing each time Felix spoke.

"*Yes*, she wants to meet me, Dad, oh my God!

98

Seriously! What is wrong with this fami.."

"Is she deranged, Felix? Does she know that you're currently trying desperately to base your entire persona on a heroin addict who hasn't been alive for the best part of half a century? Is she *stupid*, or something? Felix? Is that what's happening? Are you doing voluntary work or something?"

Felix, leg numb from dangling awkwardly through the window, felt his mouth fall open, too numb to find words and feeling incredibly stupid.

Muttering something about 12-hour shifts and a complete lack of respect, Felix's father walked into the house, still shaking his head.

Shuffling, and feeling about six years old, Felix inched his way back into the bedroom.

Pausing for nothing, not even the mirror, he ran through the open bedroom door, down the stairs and into the street. With seconds to spare, the evening bus into town pulled up, picked him up, and continued on its journey.

In the centre of town, outside the Grand Old Duke pub, Carla was completely failing at trying not to shiver in the rain.

Mid 20's but hoping to look no older than 20 to each man she stared at, she lit a cigarette while simultaneously stubbing its predecessor out under a heel.

She sniffed hard and her nose made a squeak that, thankfully, she'd never managed to make around a guy or at work.

Stepping further into the shelter to protect her deliberately uninspired blue jeans and woollen jacket from the wind and rain, she leaned her head to the left and let out a depressed sigh as it rested on the corrugated wall.

"Dates." She muttered to herself. "*Real* dates. What am I *doing*?"

She was looking at the steady early evening traffic rolling slowly past the pub when a blue and silver bus dragged to a halt on the opposite side of the road. When it pulled away a few seconds later, there stood the black-clad figure of a slight-framed man. He was fiddling with his hair but stopped the moment he saw her.

"That's him," she sighed under her breath, "Carla, I bet you any fucking money that it's him."

The figure caught her gaze and, putting his hands deep into his pockets and as far away from his hair as possible, He walked with a deliberately slow stride across the road to where Carla stood, breaking into a slightly scared run for a split second when a car zoomed near.

"You must be Carla," he said. "Are you Carla?"

"Felix," Carla replied, with a half-faked smile. "Yes. Hello. Thanks for coming."

Thanks for coming, Carla thought. Christ, where did *that* come from? She wasn't actually grateful for his presence at first sight, and, as usual, was already preparing to scold herself later for arranging a date with a moron.

"Didn't think I was gonna make it," he deliberately slurred, plucking a bent, flattened Marlboro packet from his jeans and lighting one. "Parents...well, *people,* I mean, giving me hell. You know. A *lot* of shit goin' on. Want one?" he said, offering the pack to her.

"No thanks," said Carla, blowing smoke in the direction of the question but still managing to smile, "I'm still smoking this one. We gonna go in, then?"

Felix frowned momentarily. She didn't seem impressed by his presence in the way that women seemed impressed by guys in Netflix movies. He thought she looked more *de*pressed than *im*pressed. Ignoring the thought, or trying to, he replaced the frown with a smile, nodded, and held an arm towards the door to indicate 'after you'.

Carla rolled her eyes, sighed, and confidently flung open the pub door.

The pub was louder than Felix expected, and like Carla trying to suppress her shivers, Felix failed to contain his visible discomfort. The pair struggled through the crowd to an empty booth at the back of the room.

"You wanna drink?" asked Felix in the most deliberately-casual voice he had.

"Probably," Carla deadpanned, removing her jacket without making eye contact. Her eyes quickly darted around nearby men to see if she'd taken their attention from their friends, or, ideally, partners. They had, but only because she was suddenly staring at them. She quickly realised how obviously she was doing this and flashed a fake but convincing smile at Felix, and said: "That sounded so *bad*, haha. Yes. Thank you. I would *love* a drink, *thank* you", careful to make eye contact and flash a bigger, more encouraging smile. "Want me to pay?" she added sweetly, hoping he'd say 'no' as her purse had been eaten.

101

"No, no! It's ok! Honestly!" said Felix, waving a hand as if to dismiss the idea, "I've got this. White wine, isn't it? You say so on the dating site? White wine, right? Am I right?"

"White wine would be great," Carla replied, holding the same friendly smile, which dropped instantly when she began scrolling through her phone and typing. Felix nodded a friendly smile that she didn't see, and made his way to the bar.

'White wine, paranormal, animals, travelling, nights out and meeting new guys', he whispered, repeating the 'Hobbies & Interests' section of Carla's profile to himself like a mantra.

Returning, he placed the drinks on the table between their phones, spilling some slightly as he sat. "Ah God, shit, *sorry*," he stammered and momentarily thought of wiping the spillage with his sleeve before spotting a nearby napkin and using that instead.

"It's fine, no problem," laughed Carla, while thinking what an idiot Felix was and securing her glass from his frantic napkin-dabbing.

"I spill *everything*, I really do," said Felix while mopping the mess, "My dad says…well…it doesn't matter what he says," he continued, slowing his movements as he sat back down. "My dad's a dick," said Felix, hoping he sounded cool. "Is your dad a dick as well?"

Carla looked as shocked as Felix at the words. "No. My dad isn't a dick, but thanks for asking," she said with a straight but clearly annoyed face.

"Sorry," stammered Felix, "I wasn't calling your dad a dick," he added needlessly, "I mean, I don't know him, do I?" Trying to dig himself out of this awkward early hole, his nerves ensured he instead dug deeper, "I mean, like, he *can't* be a dick, because *you* don't seem like a dick, and I'm sure your *mother* isn't a dick…"

Carla felt her jaw begin to drop slowly. Felix failed to notice this and continued his nervous trail of thought, seemingly unable to stop.

"I mean, she wouldn't have *married* him if he was a dick, of course…unless, she was a dick *too*, and, like I say, she's probably not either, because you're clearly n…"

Carla's jaw fell so low that it looked ready to disjoint from her skull, and her eyebrows raised. Felix finally noticed, but continued.

"No it's ok, I'm not saying your *mom* is a dick, *or* your dad I wasn't…look *nobody* is a dick, ok? I didn't call anyone a dick, oh God Felix stop saying 'Dick', for Christ's sake…" Felix paused for breath and looked at Carla, who was now smiling slightly, but trying not to show it.

"Look, I..I'll shut up, ok? Sorry. I mean shut up completely, I'll just stop talking about your parents and stop saying 'Dick."

Carla laughed, "It's fine, she said," raising a hand to her giggling mouth and lightly dismissing his apology with the other, "Really, it's fine. They're not dicks, and I'm not a dick", she smiled.

"I know, sorry. I'm not normally like this on dates, I promise. Just had a crazy day. Look. How are you?" Felix said, to change the subject. He realised that things weren't playing out the way they had in the roughly twenty thousand run-throughs of this moment he'd had since the date was arranged via messages.

"I'm fine," said Carla, accepting the new topic, "Mad day with my dog, and my mum, but…"

"Aw, you've got a dog?" said Felix, suddenly feeling as if he could get over his lifelong hatred of animals in a heartbeat on hearing her words, "I *love* dogs," he added, "I had to get mine back from the vet earlier, that's why I was nearly late…and…I love paranormal things and travelling and parties and things like that, too". Carla didn't hear his soft, self-conscious voice.

"Yeah, *he* can be a dick sometimes," she continued, nodding solemnly. Felix nodded, too.

"My mum wants us to get rid of him. He makes me sneeze. But I can't, I love him too much. I mean, I only *have* him because one of the women at work woke up to a kitchen full of puppies one morning and…"

"Work?" Interrupted Felix when he heard the word, "You've got a job? What about college?"

Carla looked momentarily puzzled, momentarily forgetting she was supposed to be nineteen, and then, for a moment that felt like an hour, felt incredibly guilty.

"Oh!" she said, regaining her composure, "Yes…I…I meant part-time, around college, erm…waitress work. I'm a waitress. Part-time, yes, only at weekends because, yes, because of…of college." She smiled, remembering her story, "I go to college. That's definitely what I do".

"Great! That's great!" said Felix, "Wow, studying law all week and then earning money around it, that's so cool," he smiled.

"It is when your fat doggo isn't eating it," she said with an arched eyebrow, sliding her glass a little further away from the still-wet section of the table.

"Not his fault though," she added, before changing the subject, "What about you? How's life in a punk band?"

This was Felix's moment, he thought. The time he had been waiting for. The time he had practiced for hours each night all week in his bedroom mirror, with the poster of Sid Vicious looming large behind and in front of him. This was it. Exactly as rehearsed, he slid down slightly in his seat and placed an outstretched arm along the back of his side of the booth. Having recently Googled the word 'wistful' after hearing it in a movie, he then attempted to look wistfully towards the bar.

"It is what it is," he said, his facial muscles uniting on cue in an attempt to portray wistfulness a little while longer.

"What does that mean? asked Carla with a frown, "And what's wrong with your face?"

Felix's self-conscious posture returned quickly to its original rigid position. He coughed nervously.

"I mean, it's, y'know, it's…good", he said, "Although you could easily get *wistful* about it, to be honest. I often do. That's what I was doing just now."

"Oh! Oh. That sounds…cool," offered Carla.

Felix nodded. "Yeah, it gets a little hectic you know, but it pays the bills, and it keeps a roof over my head, I guess," again, he added a practiced smile and nod at his drink as he spoke.

"Oh, you have your own place?" asked Carla quickly.

"Um, yep," said Felix, fairly quietly. "Mm-hm. My own place. Yep. I mean, yes, sure, of course… my *pad*, my…apartment?"

Carla didn't notice his voice rise to a question, "Wow, she said. That's great! I mean, I do too, of course. Stopped living with my mum and dad *years* ago, but wow, yeah, that's great!"

Felix smiled at Carla's smile and the news of her independence. His desperate little mind instantly flooded with images of him striding into her sleek penthouse apartment like a rockstar, ready for a debauched night of fun with this dream woman, and staggering home in the morning. He raised the double glass of white wine to his mouth and swallowed it all like a thirsty dog. His face burst into a repulsed shiver which, unexpected as it was, he managed to contain and minimise.

"You ok?" asked Carla with a frown again.

Felix felt the vile shiver linger around his head, and the room began to blur slightly.

"Yes, I'm fine", he said quietly loudly with a beaming smile, "So! Your own apartment huh? Wow, waitress work must pay well, and it must be great to study your college course without parents around and all that stuff".

"You mentioned your dad earlier?" said Carla, steering away from the subject, "Does he live with you, your dad?"

Felix looked horrified at the question and had to struggle in his newly-blurred state to deliver his answer.

"Oh, you mean in my apartment? My great big apartment? And my Dad? Erm...yes," he stuttered, "I mean no...well, he *did*, but...but he's really really ill and stuff like that, so they thought it best if...and yeah so he's in a hospital now, umm...a private hospital, type of thing, that I...pay for...with my…punk band…money? So, yeah", said Felix, his lies trailing off as the room spun slightly.

"Aw," said Carla, looking at Felix in the same way she looked at her dog, "A punk with a heart, eh", she smiled warmly.

Felix gulped at the sight but remained calm. "Yep, he said, that's me," and repeated his attempt to look wistfully towards the bar.

"You sure you're ok?" Carla asked him, looking more concerned than last time.

Felix felt momentarily stupid again and decided to stop trying to look wistful for the rest of the evening.

"Yes, I'm fine, just thinking about old dad," he said, "In…you know…the private hospital that I pay a lot of money for. But anyway, enough about me," Felix reached for the wine bottle and poured himself another full glass. Noticing that Carla's glass was

still more or less full, he placed the bottle next to his own glass instead of returning it to the centre of the table.

Carla's nodded, looking slightly sad, "So caring," she whispered with a smile, placing her hand on top of his in the centre of the table.

Felix, holding his glass, instantly downed the double without taking his eyes off Carla.

"Yep, he said, I'm…that…yes, thanks", he said as he felt her warm hand pulse on top of his. She slowly withdrew it, and Felix felt a rush of pride at realising his hand didn't shake at her touch.

"So…" he said, growing confident in his ability to feel a woman's touch without making a quivering fool of himself, and feeling that his blood was slowly being replaced by the cheapest white wine the barmaid had, "Those pictures and videos you sent...they really you, then?" he left his hand on the table in case her touch returned, but it didn't.

Carla glanced briefly around the room, "Yes," she half whispered with a confident, devilish smile, "Of course they are. Why, did you like them, then?"

Felix felt a rush of wine or something hormonal flood through his body and instantly answered, "Yes," with a crack in his voice.

"I mean," he said after a slight cough, "Yes, I did. Very nice." As casually as he could manage, he moved his abandoned hand from the centre of the table and picked up the bottle again, filling his glass once more to the brim until it slightly overflowed. Felix didn't notice the new spillage as he nervously grabbed the glass and began to drink.

"And what about you?" Carla asked. Noticing the small amount of wine left in the bottle, she downed her drink and refilled her glass with the remainder. A passing waitress caught her eye and nodded as Carla indicated for another bottle.

"Those pictures of yours, is that really you?" she asked, raising an optimistic eyebrow subconsciously as she felt the wine hit her head hard.

"Yep," said Felix, placing his near-empty glass on the table and feeling his face glow, grin, and distort uncontrollably, "I work on my abs every day. Three times, some days. All me...why, did you like them?"

Carla grinned and nodded as the waitress appeared, placed an open bottle and new bill on the table, and left. Felix refilled his glass and removed his leather jacket as a sudden wave of sweat and nausea rocked his body and made the room sway. An awkward silence filled their booth.

This is it, thought Felix, almost aloud due to his

excitement. His mind quickly raced through his bedroom preparations for inevitable small talk. He knew he had to keep her interested. He knew he had to *show* interest in her and *keep* her interested in himself. Feeling in control, his mind calmly recalled images of her ever-changing dating profile and the most recent entries under her 'Hobbies' section, namely 'paranormal' and 'animals'.

With regrettably little hesitation, Felix leaned forward with a raised eyebrow, his face moodily lit by the wall lamp, and half-whispered: "My dog and I both had diarrhea – *at the same time,"* ending the sentence with a look of shock, a slow nod and the whispered words, "Twice. *Spooky".*

Carla looked mortified. Drunk, but mortified.

"Eerm, *what*?" she asked, "Did you just say…"

Felix instantly regretted the comment and interrupted her words, in an attempt to change the subject to something less ridiculous.

"Do you like Sid Vicious?" he slurred, failing in his attempt, as his free wobbling hand tried to casually spike his hair.

"Who? Is he an actor?" asked Carla, in genuine uncertainty, watching Felix's hand as it quickly twisted a chunk of hair, pulling it to a point briefly before it flopped back down and resumed looking like a large slug on his head.

"He was a *punk*," said Felix, slapping the table for emphasis a lot louder than he'd have liked to.

"Oh, cool!" said Carla, hoping to look knowledgeable on the new topic, and now picturing Felix's penthouse lined with expensive, exclusive, limited edition lithographs of musical greats and photographs of Felix hanging out with rock legends.

109

"What did he do?" asked Carla genuinely.

"He did...punk things," said Felix with a nod, hoping that would be enough.

"Oh. Like what?" Carla asked further.

Felix looked vacant as he thought for an answer. His blurry eyes found his glass and then fell back to Carla, "Like, me, y'know, being a punk and stuff. The band, and...he looked a bit like me, you know. Same hair. *Exactly* the same hair".

"Cool!" said Carla, really not knowing what to say and detecting that Felix was more than a little bit drunk.

The pair sat in silence. Carla's phone suddenly lit up, and both of their eyes fell on it. Carla noticed this, and Felix obligingly pretended to stare at his wine glass.

"Ugh," said Carla, sliding her phone screen to unlock it. "Work people. They're always bloody messaging me at weekends. They know full well that I haven't worked weekends for *years*." She rolled her eyes at Felix, filled her glass, and took a long drink.

"They can wait until *Monday*," she said with a victorious smile and placed her phone face down on the table.

Felix smiled along with her, feeling elated on some level that he wasn't expecting to feel; she had ignored *them* for *him*. It took every ounce of anxious semi-sober restraint he had to stop his face from breaking into a proud grin, and instead he filled his glass and emptied it.

"So you must meet a lot of women...with your band. Or is it solo stuff that you do?" Carla asked, filling her glass again once Felix's white finger-

110

tipped grip had finally released the bottle.

Felix pondered the question, wondering what the best answer would be.

His mind jumped forward briefly to an image of arriving home drunk later, sneaking up the trellis on the wall beneath his window, avoiding his permanently irate father and somehow sobering up. He replaced the panicked thought with a vision of somehow making it back to this college girl's penthouse apartment, and living the night of a thousand lonely fantasies.

Carla, her swaying head suddenly filled with an image of her annoying mother and their tiny home, was enjoying a similar fantasy about Felix's pad as they stared blurrily at each other and smiled.

It was then that Carla noticed, for the first time, just as Felix leaned his head back to take his latest long gulp of white wine, just how pathetic his moustache was. The light, the angle, the shadows from the bar, all conspired to show the moustache in its true form; four or five clusters of six or seven rather straggly hairs, dotted along his top lip and carefully flattened horizontally.

Carla's eyes screwed up at the sight. For a brief moment, she felt as though she felt as though she was staring at her newly-teenage cousin getting steadily drunk at a family gathering. She shook her head to break the image as Felix continued swigging from his glass.

"So," she eventually said, resting her head on her left hand and gazing at Felix, "You must meet a lot of girls" she repeated in a slurred attempt at a seductive purr that matched her blurring eyes, "How do I compare to your other teenage girls, Mr. Punk

Star?"

Felix's head was spinning now. It had been spinning for some time with a cocktail of thoughts about how drunk he was, about how he was properly drunk for the first time in his entire life, and how there was absolutely *zero* chance of his father not finding out about all of this. Now, a new thought staggered to the front of his drunken mind and eradicated his previous flashes of reality.

"She's *flirting*," Felix thought to himself as he stared at Carla.

"What?" slurred Carla. Felix, realising instantly that rather than thinking he'd actually been speaking aloud, was drunk enough to ignore her question and pursue his thought without embarrassment. His mind instantly scrolled through the last half hour of every movie he had ever seen that ended with a kiss, and every porn video that began in a bar. Ignoring his now-constant feeling of impending vomit, he mimicked her body language and, after two failed attempts, managed to rest his chin on the palm of his right hand.

"Oh, they're *nothing* compared to *you*," Felix managed to say with clarity.

"Oh *really*," responded Carla, in a successful attempt at a purr this time and curling her hair with her free index finger, "Well maybe we should…"

The pair, following each other's drunken lead, and moved their heads forward over the table until their lips met. The very moment their mouths touched, Felix's arms involuntarily shot out and across the table, sending a glass and Carla's phone to opposite ends of her booth seat.

"Oh my God!" shouted Felix, shocked briefly into

sobriety.

"Ah! Gasped Carla, quickly checking that her phone was safe and the glass had been empty, "No harm done. Phew!" she smiled, before laughing. She turned to smile at Felix as a reminder of their moment before his random arm spasm, ready to pick up where they left off. Felix continued smiling to himself, a look that beamed with pride more than happiness, as he poured them both a full glass of wine.

He shoved her glass towards her and quickly drank half of his own.

"Wow," he said, sitting back in the chair and bearing an almost post-orgasmic grin of joy. He raised a glass as if to say 'cheers', before adding, "Thank you. Seriously, like, *seriously,* though, thank you," before attempting to drink the rest of his wine.

Carla laughed and felt herself blush. Her hand began to rise to her mouth again but reached for her glass instead. "That good, am I?" she said, as she emptied her glass in a torrent of unashamedly loud gulps.

"The *best*," said Felix, momentarily forgetting his image for the first time in years and looking suddenly even more like a grinning schoolboy than when Carla had first noticed the light hit his facial hair two drinks ago.

His now-boyish figure suddenly began bobbing as he continued his happy tirade. Carla laughed at the sight of him bobbing around with all the excitement of a child on Christmas morning.

"Wow," she laughed, slightly self-consciously as Felix continued his strange excited gestures. She glanced around the room, feeling suddenly awkward

113

as one or two people began to look over at Felix's gleeful, bouncing figure.

"Erm, thank you?" she finally offered. Her drunken impulsive mood was being rapidly replaced by a feeling of complete embarrassment, without being quite sure why.

"Haha, no thank *you*!" laughed Felix, finally stopping his joyful seated dance, but not his trail of thought, "I'm gonna be the talk of the school on Monday," he beamed, "I'm gonna be all over Instagram!"

The words confused Carla on many levels. Her first thought was that Felix had been saying that he worked as a musician, not in a school.

Secondly, and just as confusingly to her, *why would he be the talk of the school?* His words suggested some kind of trouble arising from their date, but his beaming face and breaking voice suggested nothing but absolute joy. Happiness. *Victory,* even.

Carla's smile left her face as she stared, puzzled, at Felix, who had reached for his phone and was frantically typing away. Panicked thoughts filled her mind…*Is he a part-time college teacher? Did he think she was a student at the college he teaches at? Had she chosen the wrong fake backstory?*

"What…what do you mean?" Carla managed, now holding a fake smile in the same way that she did for selfies. Her eyes darted around the room again and saw more people turning to look at Felix's strange and increasingly childlike movements.

"Felix, *Felix!*" she repeated, shouting slightly. He looked up from his phone and turned his head to face hers, still grinning.

114

"What do you mean, Felix?" she asked calmly, trying to maintain a smile, "And what's with the silly dancing?" she giggled deliberately, reaching out a subtle hand to his arm in an attempt to stop his movements.

"Eh?" Felix grinned, feeling drunk now on a sudden first feeling of maturity more than white wine.

"Oh!" he said, finally remembering his recent words and movements. "I just mean, at school on Monday! I'm the only kid in my class, probably the *year*, to be honest, who's never been drunk, never

kissed a girl, *all* of it, but not now! Ha! Thank you *so, so* much for this! I can't wait to see your penthouse!"

Carla's face fell. For a moment she was too numb to speak, too stunned to comprehend Felix's words or process them enough to respond.

"Wuh...Wha..." she finally grunted with a heavy breath, feeling as though every bit of air in her lungs had just been punched out of her. Felix carried on drinking, typing and giggling, occasionally pausing to upload a quick photo of his glass or the table or the lipstick trace on his fluffy moustache. He quickly pointed his phone's camera lens toward Carla, and the flash of light caused her to blink hard and sober up fast.

"What did you say, Felix?" Carla said the words calmly like a school teacher, and then barked, "Felix! What did you just say about school? *School?*"

Felix's grin dropped to a small smile as he placed his phone back in his jacket pocket. He had no idea when he had started telling Carla the truth about himself, but realising that's what was happening and drunkenly deciding that she didn't sound very angry, he continued to speak.

"Yeah, yeah," he nodded, "Plus, all the other lads in my class have only kissed girls out of our grade! Never *older* girls! I know for a *fact* that I'm the only boy in my year to have kissed a 19-year-old girl! Wow!" Felix grinned at Carla. Carla looked horrified.

"Sooo…", Felix continued, his hand making a feeble attempt to secure the wine bottle. Failing, he rested his head on the palm of his hand on his first attempt this time. Realising that this move took only one attempt despite how drunk he presently was, Felix felt even more grown up than when their lips briefly touched.

"What happens now, then?" he asked, "Is that it? Are we…y'know…*dating* now?"

Carla looked horrified. "Whu…Wha…what?" she breathed.

"Am I dating a 19-year-old? Is that, like, is that *it*, now?" Felix asked, smiling like an optimistic child arriving at a funfair, "Where do we go now? Do we go back to your penthouse apartment thing?"

He began to bounce in excitement again. Carla ignored it.

"Felix," Carla asked in a firm, flat, hard voice, before adding in words she really couldn't believe she was having to say, "How old are you?"

The long pause she expected didn't come. "Fourteen," beamed Felix instantly, resuming his celebratory dance and responding to a flurry of sudden messages on his phone.

"I'm..I'm sorry, *what*?" gasped Carla with genuine disbelief despite the facial hair clues she had noticed but had been trying not to think about since the second bottle arrived.

"Basically *fifteen*, though," added Felix, "Fifteen in the summer holidays," he smiled politely and began typing frantically into his phone screen, grinning again as he did so.

"What?" shouted Carla as the boy's words finally and fully dawned on her, "You're *fourteen?*" she gasped.

"Yyyep," beamed Felix, "I am a proper *punk*, though," he added, "I mean, I will be, when I leave school. But I've got the same hair as Sid, and..." he tugged at his jacked and smiled at her.

"Oh my God," she stammered, "You...your profile said you were 25," and a look of abject disgust swept across her face. Carla's hands loosened the collar of her sweater as a sudden wave of sweat and wine consumed her.

"A lot of lads in my class say I look 25," Felix added proudly, nodding at his own words, "Here," he said, leaning his face towards her and tilting it upwards, "I've got a moustache, see? I mean, you have to get in the light a bit to see it but...look, can you see it? I mean, I basically *look* 25, so...and who's going to want to meet a 14-year-old boy?" he laughed.

"Oh Jesus Christ," stammered Carla as her head began to shake from side to side.

She glanced around the room in panic as if waking from an operation she hadn't been aware of. Felix finally began to sense her horror and his smile dropped again. He reached a hand across the table to her, an action of consoling a loved one that he'd seen guys make in restaurants when his mother took him for Valentine's Day meals or to celebrate his mid-term exam results.

"Babe," Felix said, "What's wrong? You know you

117

can talk to me, right?"

Carla's body froze in shock at what was happening.

"Is it the age thing?" asked Felix, "Look, you're nineteen, I'm nearly fifteen, I'm sorry for lying about my age, but those sites don't let you join if...and when you think about it, in a few years from now, I'll be..."

Carla snatched his hand from her arm and slammed it into the table. She wiped the hand that touched him on her jeans as if wiping away blood and looked at Felix in horror. Seeing Felix's still-joyful smile and attempt at compassion, her face fell into an angry frown.

"I'm...I'm twenty-five," she confessed in a suppressed roar, her eyes scanning the room again in horror at her situation.

"Wh...*what?*" stammered Felix, his ridiculous grin finally leaving his face. "I said I'm twenty-fucking-five, you little embryo, I'm a fucking *lawyer* not a bloody *student*..." she hissed in disgust at them both, "I said I was nineteen on that bloody stupid app because every guy on that app is chasing young girls and you don't stand a chance unless you lie about your..." her eyes raised to meet Felix's puzzled gaze and her confession stopped. The look of disgust and horror fell across her face again.

"Why the hell am I telling *you* this, she spat, "Oh my *God*, I'm gonna be sick" she said with her voice cracking as her eyes scanned her body in self-loathing before falling back on Felix.

Felix stared back blankly.

"You're...you're twenty-five?" he finally asked.

"Yes," Carla responded, out of breath, feeling

exhausted by shock.

The two stared at each other for a moment longer.

"Oh *God*," Carla exclaimed, still looking shell-shocked, "I'm actually going to throw up, oh my God".

The weight of events suddenly fully hit her for the first time, "Oh my fucking God I just kissed a child," she said as her hand suddenly flew to cover her mouth, "Our lips touched, I'm gonna be *sick.*" Her hand tightened its grip across her mouth and her eyes reluctantly fell on Felix's again.

"Oh God, I'm gonna be *arrested*," she said in a horrified panic.

"Oh God, I'm gonna be a *hero*!" beamed Felix slamming his hand on the table deliberately, causing several groups of standing drinkers to glance in their direction, "At school on Monday, they'll all be like, 'Oh yeah, I was out with this girl from the next year up at the weekend, blah blah blah', and I'll be like, 'Oh yeah? Oh *yeah*? Well, my girlfriend is twenty-five and we kissed in a pub and she's got this penthouse apartment, and she's a lawyer waitress and…"

"We didn't kiss and I'm not a fucking waitress," snapped Carla instantly defending herself.

Felix looked crestfallen.

"Didn't we?" he asked, looking suddenly sad.

"We absolutely did not," said Carla in an exasperated tone. "And I'm certainly not your bloody *girlfriend,* you little idiot…our lips touched, that wasn't a *kiss*…we both drank a lot and we nearly…" she paused her rant as her eyes focused on the fluff along his top lip, "The moustache, why didn't I see your pathetic fluffy moustache? You are so clearly a

119

child, oh my God what the hell am I doing…" she asked herself, reaching for her phone to put into her shoulder bag on the seat next to her.

"We *didn't?*" asked Felix again, looking completely deflated. His hand ignored his spiked hair and began trying to gently fluff his moustache into volume and existence.

"No, we bloody didn't!" shouted Carla, "and if…" her eyes scanned the room to make sure nobody was staring again before she hissed with a pointed finger, "And if you say one bloody word about this to your little friends or do anything with that picture of me I'll…" Carla, now feeling fully sober, glanced Felix up and down in complete disgust.

"I'll *tell your dad!* I'll *sue* you, you little shit." Carla grabbed her bag and rose to her feet, wiping her mouth for the fifth time and doing her best to calmly storm out, tears of anger and humiliation in her eyes.

Felix sat at the table alone. Suddenly, his phone beeped again.

The notification from his dating app informed him that his membership would expire in one week. Realising that he hadn't got his father's credit card details with him, the boy swiped the notification away.

Rising to his feet, staggering slightly, he swayed his way across the bar until the cold outdoor air hit him, briefly wiping details of the night's event from his mind as it did so. He felt sober and stupid.

Glancing down the street, dimly lit by clubs, wine bars, and generic crowds of other pretty little liars, he could just make out Carla's huddled and probably-weeping figure slowly entering a bus doorway. The doors closed behind her as she boarded the vehicle, and it drove slowly away in the opposite direction to where the penthouse apartments stood.

Felix's phone beeped again. Opening the message from his father, he saw fifteen others preceding it. They initially informed the rebel of his bedtime that night and the national average curfew time for a boy of his age. The messages then descended into a stream of parental orders detailing Felix's new, even earlier curfew and bedtimes, with a new list of household chores and confiscated gadgets, toys and posters.

Felix sighed and looked at his reflection in a large puddle on the road in front of him. It reminded him of someone, it reminded him of his bedroom poster. The shape was there, the jacket was there, and the silhouette of the scuffed boots was perfect. But inside that rainy, rippling silhouette, on the side of Felix's image that was grimly covered by reality and daily life, Felix saw in the reflection a child, desperate to be anyone but himself, with an expensive phone full of angry messages from a very annoying but ultimately loving father and an entire persona that belonged to someone else.

Felix sighed at the reflection in the puddle. With perfect timing, after making a couple of stops around the town, Carla's bus ploughed through the puddle, on towards the housing estates, and completely soaked Felix in the process.

The sound of adult laughter rang out from the people exiting the bar behind him. Felix, crying now, turned around to look at them briefly and thought of asking them for help, or a hug. Turning back to the empty spot where the puddle and his silhouette had been, he removed the tin-gold rings from each of his fingers. Noticing the black bands they had left around each of his digits, he dropped them onto the floor and quickly bundled his hands into his pockets and began to walk home quickly, suddenly feeling like the lost schoolboy he was.

Three hours later, back in his bedroom after returning via the back door to prepare his nightly glass of warm milk, Felix Butler, currently undisturbed by his livid father, lay fast asleep.

On a wooden chair in a tiny kitchen on the other side of town, next to a fat, indifferent dog, Carla Porter sat at a table removing what little makeup her tears hadn't washed away. Pausing the flood long enough to send a short, late-night "Hey stranger, I was just thinking of u ;)" to literally every guy behind her reinstated social media accounts, she turned crying again to her dog, who raised a slow, unbothered eyebrow and did nothing else. Confused, sad, and feeling older than ever, Carla deleted the dating app, switched off her phone and snored for nine hours, chorused by the dog on the kitchen floor.

The next morning, head spinning, Felix reached for his phone before his eyes were fully open, as usual.

Opening up the dating app he instantly clicked on his profile icon. He saw his boyish moustache. He saw the crudely cropped and heavily filtered profile photo of his well-lit facial hair attempt, which just about chopped his school uniform from view. He looked at his puffy, pale young cheeks, and his awful hair, and glanced at his age. Twenty-five. He momentarily realised how lucky he had been in not being reported on one of the many times he had swiped right.

Clicking 'Edit', a new menu popped up. Felix stared at the new options. His head began to ache and throb as a brief look of embarrassment filled his face. In a sudden move, Felix deleted a string of profile text and typed a few new letters.

"There," his alcohol-cracked voice croaked with a slight smile, "Nineteen. *Much* more convincing," and with that, he reached for a note hidden beneath his mattress, typed the numbers from his father's credit card into the app, closed his phone, dropped it to the floor, and fell back to sleep.

Faithless

Reverence

The rain was showing no signs of stopping or even slowing when Adam broke his gaze to look at his watch. It was ten to five on a Wednesday afternoon.

He was standing watching it pour outside the window in much the same manner as he had been for God knows how long; watching droplets gather from patches to puddles, watching slated rooftops seemingly get darker as they steadily saturated, watching stray dogs carrying on regardless.

Watching the schoolchildren walking home at what must have been about four o'clock was pretty funny, he found, as they all, by and large, had no coats. The boys with their soggy twisted shirt collars and their shoelaces dragging alongside in puddles. The girls with their matted hair, waterlogged ankle socks and pink, blotchy, freezing cold legs.

It struck Adam as somehow disappointing that even though these children were surely no older than, say, eleven, they all seemed to harbour the idea that running home would make them look like babies.

"They can't *all* be strays," said Adam, his first spoken thought for well over an hour.

"What?" said Sara, still sitting on the edge of the bed but no longer staring into oblivion.

She hated the way she answered him. Not the resigned, uninterested tone of her voice; she'd been planning that ever since she realised he'd gone into one of his silent moods. What she hated was the fact that her well-planned, couldn't-care-less attitude had been wasted by showing interest. She hadn't spoken for so long either that when she replied, her voice cracked, making it sound weak, timid, and upset. Although this was exactly how she felt, she didn't want Adam to know it.

"The dogs," Adam repeated. "I've seen seven now, I think, or eight, and they can't *all* be homeless."

Sara ignored him. Realising that now he'd broken his silence he'd soon turn to face her, she began picking at her nails, concentrating on each loose flap of skin as hard as she could. She was still as eager to prove her disinterest, but could not risk her voice failing on her twice.

"Even if they *are* homeless," Adam continued, "and I still don't think they *are*, by the way...well they must be pretty fucking stupid. It's pissing down out there, and they just walk around, pissing up the same bit of fence. They haven't even got the sense to sit under a fucking *bush* or something. Jesus Christ."

Sara left her fingers alone.

"That's what dogs *do*, you fool," she suddenly snapped back. "Dogs don't mind the rain. And anyway, even if they did, they couldn't hide under a bush because they'd be too big. You meant to say "Hide under a tree."

"Well, under a fucking tree then"

"Couldn't. Still, get wet from the branches"

Sara couldn't help but smile as she said this, and she knew that Adam would be able to tell she was smiling from the tone of her smooth, fully recovered voice. This made her smile to herself even more so.

"Does this mean we're speaking again?" she said.

Adam stayed silent for a few seconds. "I wasn't aware that we'd stopped," he said finally.

Sara leaned back on the bed, throwing her weight onto her forearms, "Well, *I* hadn't".

Ignoring his verbal dig, Sara just felt relieved that Adam didn't take her response in the way it had unintentionally sounded; - sarcastic, aloof.

Instead, he turned from the window and gave his eyes several long, hard blinks as they adjusted from the rain to the room. Sara watched him through pink sunglasses. Before they were arguing, they had been playing around with the sunglasses as well as hats and clothes which they had found when a chest of drawers collapsed during the fight earlier.

Sara had kept the glasses on throughout the argument for the same reason as she was now, as an act of defiance. A great big "Fuck You" to greet him every time he turned to face her.

Adam walked over to the bookshelf, quite aware of the fact that she would be watching him, and picked up a cigarette from an already opened packet. He lit it, taking a long, deep, relieving drag before loudly exhaling a perfectly random cloud of smoke.

"What happens now then?" said Sara, admitting to herself the point scoring was over she removed the glasses.

Adam turned again to face the window but remained standing by the bookcase. He took another drag on his cigarette and leaned his head back to rest on the books. Slowly and softly he began to whisper "And left behind/arms full of life / and all this useless beauty".

"What?" said Sara.

"Remember that?" said Adam, still not looking at her.

"'Course," she said. "That poem you wrote about me".

Adam laughed to himself.

"Yes! And I always loved it, but said I didn't understand the bit about my arms" said Sara, as if she had to prove that she remembered it. Adam sniggered a second time as smoke bellowed from his mouth, and he dropped the subject as quickly as he'd introduced it.

"Still raining, then," he said instead.

"Christ." Sara was beginning to crack under what she thought were Adam's little games against her. She sat bolt upright on the bed, leaning her body towards him as she finally cracked and shouted. "Fuck the rain, fuck the dogs and tell me what the fuck we are supposed to do now?"

"You're wrong, you know, I mean, you do know you're wrong don't you? You do realise that?" Said Adam calmly, finally looking at her eye to eye.

"Who...What?" breathed Sara, startled by his detachment and his calm. Besides this, any kind of shouting always left her breathless.

"About the rain. You are wrong about the rain."

"H...How do you mean I'm wro..."

"All that bullshit about dogs loving it!" screamed Adam, leaning up from the bookcase towards her, waving his cigarette arm through the air while his other hand was thrust a fist into his trouser pocket. "Of course they fucking don't!"

Sara stood up to face Adam eye to eye and at close range, determined to be entitled to her opinion. "And how do you know that a dog might not like the rain? Dogs have feelings, just like people. I *love* the rain, you know I do," she hugged herself gently and smiled at Adam, her voice growing softer as she recalled a happier time.

"The night we met," she purred, "the rain was absolutely…"

"Let me tell you this" shouted Adam, walking to within a few inches of her "This, right, *all* of this what you're about to say right now, is bullshit. Don't keep banging on about walking home from work on a Friday in the rain, grinning like some fucking moron,

128

or about when we were walking back from the cinema at half one in the morning and it started to piss it down, and you said about how it was all perfect and you didn't care that you had no fucking hood, because that's just *bullshit*, that is. It's wet, it's cold, and you end up ill for a fucking week. So don't stand there saying that. There's not a single person alive who likes the rain, and anyone who says differently is a fucking liar".

They stared at each other for a short while, neither blinking. Adam was not sure whether he expected Sara to reply or not. He felt as if he should feel guilty for shouting at her in that way over such a pointless little thing as this, but he couldn't. Or rather he wouldn't. Anything to rid himself of any trace of guilt or blame.

Sara made a face of deep disgust towards Adam whilst shaking her head. She gave a little laugh to herself and turned away, slowly folding her arms.

"And what's that supposed to mean?" said Adam, desperate to say something, anything aggressive.

Sara walked a few paces away for safety before turning around to face him again. She went to unfold her arms before stopping, realising she could handle talking to him a lot better behind some kind of wall.

"We...." she said calmly, with a distant expression on her face, "are in a situation that I couldn't wish on my worst enemy, deeper in it than anyone could ever fucking imagine, and all you do is shout about the rain." She smiled an unnerving grin as she concluded her sentence, and shrugged her shoulders. Adam stayed silent, not taking the cold stare from his eyes, yet somehow trying to make it look more accessible. He sniffed loudly.

"We haven't got a clue what's going to happen to either of us, have we? Have we?" Sara added in the same calm tone.

She raised her eyebrows and reached for a cigarette from the opened packet, knowing full well that Adam wouldn't tell her to put it back for once. She didn't light it, though; she just let it dangle from her mouth. The room fell silent again, but both of them knew that it wouldn't last.

Adam took this time to think up a reply, or a reason. An excuse for his behaviour. He couldn't do it. It had all felt right at the time. Instead, he pulled his lighter from his pocket and pressed the small, plastic switch. Sara heard the noise and spun around to light her cigarette, arms still folded. Her eyes briefly fell onto his before concentrating on the orange flame. She inhaled deeply in the silence and, for effect, blew a large smoke ring above Adams' head.

"We need to talk," she said, matter-of-factly and without blinking.

Adam was not used to this He knew that whenever he acted purposely detached from the situation, whenever he had made Sara upset in some way; he was always somehow in control of her. He knew that after making her shout back at him she'd cry, then he'd console her, she'd admit he was right all along, and then everything would be alright. But it didn't get that far this time. She didn't even cry. She simply told the truth, and Adam felt weak.

Sara walked over to the newly collapsed chest of drawers and pushed it with her middle finger. It wobbled slightly but did not fall over. Adam stubbed his cigarette out in the empty ashtray. He knew it was his turn to speak, and he knew that this was his cue. Just as Sara's role had changed, so had his. He was now the timid one.

"I...I didn't expect it to turn out like this, I… "

"Well join the fucking club!" screamed Sara, turning to face him.

"Well you not exactly blameless yourself, you know," shouted Adam, his momentary lapse into timidity leaving him for good, and in the same moment he picked up the ashtray and threw it heavily along the ground. Sara's body braced at the sound; partly shocked though only slightly, and partly because she was sick of standing with her arms folded.

"Since it's all about blame," she screamed, "Let's not forget which bastard had the idea!"

Adam strode across the room, again standing inches from Sara. He didn't give her time to fold her arms.

"And let's not forget which bitch drove him to it again!" Adam shouted, his face growing purple, his vocal cords almost tearing, "Let's not forget the bitch

131

who left him with no fucking choice but to fucking do it!"

Sara could feel her weakness returning, and her thin body began to shake. "I didn't make you do a damn fucking thing" she screamed through tears. Somehow, the sound of her own screams was making her cry. She shoved him as she kept repeating herself over and over. She could hear Adam shouting something at her as she pushed and punched at him harder and harder, but she could not hear him for the sound of her own screaming.

Adam suddenly realised Sara was crying. Hard. As usual, he felt angry with her for doing this. Grabbing her by the upper arms he spun her around, tossing her across the room and onto the bed. She landed on the bed without a bounce; arms and legs flailing madly, body heaped and twisted. Adam strode across to the bookshelves, skimming books onto the floor with his right hand. Sara cried even more, even louder.

"You bastard!" she screamed, now kneeling up on the bed "You bastard! You've fucking killed us!"

Adam strode across the room, punching walls, and kicking furniture before finally stamping the disabled drawers to the ground. With this, Sara screamed louder than she had ever needed to scream before. The fear this gave her was almost unreal.

Adam banged open the door and stormed out into the hallway. He stopped still. In the back of his mind, he could hear Sara's harrowing cries, but they suddenly seemed so far away, as if they had nothing to do with him. His stare and his mind were now fixed on the wooden door ahead of him at the end of the hallway. The door he had purposely closed and locked late last night. He stared at it for a few moments longer, thinking nothing, knowing exactly what to do. Adam walked down the hall slowly, breathing heavily through his nose.

Fumbling in his shirt pocket for the key, he unlocked the door gently, silently. Sara was still wailing in the background, but that was nothing to do with him anymore.

As soon as he heard the lock click he eased open the door and walked inside the room. Turning, he locked the door behind him, placing the key back into his shirt pocket. Reaching down towards the pale corpse of the elderly tenant whose cold stiff hand was still clutching the key to her wall safe, Adam picked up his pistol from the floor, examined it briefly, and fired a single shot directly through his heart.

The room was dark when Sara finally woke. She woke in the same crumpled position she had fallen asleep in, her dress twisted around her waist. Sitting up slowly with a slight grunt she adjusted herself to the disorientated feel she always got when she woke from sleeping during the day. After yawning, she looked around the room for Adam, even though she sensed he was not there among the evening shadows.

She rubbed her face with both hands and stood upright, straightening her dress to its intended position. Leaning over the bed she lightly shoved the door until it clicked shut.

Straightening from this she slowly steered herself through the broken glass and objects scattered all over the floor and towards the window, where she stood watching the rain. In the dark street below the rain was still falling as heavily as it had been for hours. The flat rooftops in the near distance now had large puddles on them, and the lights from other windows, other lives, seemed permanently distorted through her own window. She yawned again and her jaw clicked. She felt like a child, for some reason, but that didn't seem to worry her as much as it usually did. She gave herself a slight smile, but could not think why.

Folding her thin arms protectively over the still, lifeless body inside her stomach, she leaned forward and looked at the wet, sparkling street below. The police cars, still in the same position as they had been when Adam stood at the window, had their sirens glowing but were silent now. Despite the rain, more armed officers had gathered. Their loaded guns focused red reticules on Sara, ready for the signal to shoot. During the two hours that she stood there, she didn't see a single dog.

❖❖❖

About the Author

Micheal James Bradley is an award-winning former journalist and feature writer (BBC, Birmingham Mail, Mirror Group) and is currently a full-time therapist and occasional audio book narrator.

He lives in England, somewhere, with not enough records and too many shirts. His hobbies include sleeping.

This is his first collection of both published and new short stories.

Printed in Great Britain
by Amazon

24219325R00086